DISNEY A WRINKLE IN TIME

A GUIDE TO THE UNIVERSE

Printed in the United States of America

Designed by Gegham Vardanyan

First Hardcover Edition, March 2018
1 3 5 7 9 10 8 6 4 2
ISBN 978-1-368-02296-5
FAC-008598-18019

Library of Congress Control Number on file

For more Disney Press fun, visit www.disneybooks.com

For more from the world of Disney's *A Wrinkle in Time*,
visit www.movies.disney.com/a-wrinkle-in-time

SUSTAINABLE FORESTRY INITIATIVE

Certified Sourcing
www.sfiprogram.org
SFI-00993

Logo Applies to Text Stock Only

DISNEY A WRINKLE IN TIME

A GUIDE TO THE UNIVERSE

Written by Kari Sutherland

Illustrated by VIVIEN WU

DISNEY PRESS

LOS ANGELES • NEW YORK

contents

Mrs. Which

One of three celestial beings responsible for protecting the Light from the Darkness, Mrs. Which wants nothing more than to protect and nurture the universe. She has been a warrior of the Light longer than anyone or anything can remember, and her compassion is equaled only by her radiant power.

Lights twinkled all around her, the celestial being's sisters and brothers blinking in astonishment as she hurtled through space. Dodging around a sapphire planet, she realized she'd need to go farther, as far from other life-forms as possible.

Only, her energy was lagging. The bright, fiery core of her heart was strong, but she couldn't afford to wait until she reached the fringes of the universe or she might not win. And she had to win.

She hesitated, weighing her options.

Behind her, something in the dark let out an ominous cackle, clearly thinking she was finished. No, it wasn't some*thing* in the dark; it *was* the dark—a massive, impenetrable cloud of darkness trailing her.

"Not so fast, you horrid lump," she muttered. "I'm not done yet."

Calling upon her reserves, she burst into motion, luring the evil to an open patch of space. As soon as her pursuer was clear of other objects, she doubled back.

"Let us finish this!" she called, rocketing toward it.

The creature gave a slight shake, as if surprised at her daring, but then barreled forward at full speed.

Two lights caught up to the battle and wavered on the edges, their emotions coiled in nerves as neither the Darkness nor their sister faltered—their paths clearly set on collision.

"Let the Light be enough," the first celestial

figure said to herself as the distance shrank. "Let me overcome and rise above the Darkness."

BAM!

The shudder from the impact rippled outward, knocking a planet into a new orbit, its own star reaching out to steady it as the beings on the surface dropped to the ground. The two observing figures swooped down to the clouds to help, hoping to shield the inhabitants. In the sky above, the light and the oily mass were locked together, neither moving.

"I will not let you pass!" the celestial being cried out as her light burned against the cold fingers of the dark entity, holding it back. Her green rays shifted to white as her spirit grappled with the slippery, noxious essence.

"You cannot stop me," a voice hissed. "I am everywhere, and while you weaken and fade, there is nothing that can harm me."

The light was pushed back a millimeter and the dark presence oozed in delight.

"There's no use fighting," the voice continued

smoothly. "You may as well accept me. All your worries would be over."

But she would not be fooled, and the universe meant too much to her. She had to protect it at all costs. Summoning all her hope and love for the worlds in her care, the celestial being reached out and—instead of pushing the creature back—wrapped herself around it in a fierce hug.

"No!" the voice shouted. "What are you doing?" It writhed and shook, trying to jerk free, but it was too late. The light's gravity held it tight.

Shrieking in rage, the creature flung itself at the light, lashing out at her flames, which were now a golden hue. The Darkness smothered everything it touched, violently clawing at the celestial being in an effort to force her to release it.

Implacable, she merely held the Darkness closer, allowing it to spread over her surface. The fires she kept within blossomed into orange, then a vivid scarlet as she prepared for death, the presence caught in her embrace.

"I may not be able to stop you completely, but this much I can do." She squeezed tight, feeling no pain as her heat collapsed into a pinpoint at her center. Curling smaller and smaller, the atoms compressed, their energy bunching together until they could go nowhere but out.

Ka-POW!

Light burst from the center of the celestial being, scattering the Darkness into fragments as colors shot into space between the cracks, illuminating the nearby planet like a second sun and wiping out any shadows on its surface.

The sister figures below gasped in awe.

The younger of the two quivered and asked, "Will she be okay?"

Words were harder for the second figure to manage. She searched for a quote to sum up her feelings.

" 'A thing of beauty is a joy forever; its loveliness increases; it will never pass into nothingness.' Keats, English," she finally replied.

WhOOSh!

A loud roar shook the sky as the light and darkness spooling out were suddenly sucked backward, toward the celestial being's vortex.

With a final *pop*, the light was extinguished, and all that was left was a dark gray orb, its surface pitted with craters. It hung motionless.

Crouched in the clouds of the closest planet, the younger figure sobbed, her heart aching.

"It's all right, my dear," a harmonious voice chimed as a translucent wisp of air brushed her side. "I knew the price going in and I was happy to make the sacrifice to slow the IT down."

"Slow the IT down? But . . . you defeated it. You trapped it here!" the youngest figure insisted.

But the other visible figure shook her head.

"'The battle line between good and evil runs through the heart of every man.' Solzhenitsyn, Russian," she intoned solemnly.

"What she means is that the Darkness has already infiltrated many parts of the universe, and what we

have done here today is not enough to vanquish the IT entirely," the invisible presence clarified.

"But then, why?" the youngest asked, her voice vibrating in sadness.

"We are what we do, and it is not our words but our acts that matter," the oldest being replied, her voice bold and strong despite the fact that she had given up her corporeal form for now. "It is contained as much as possible. The IT may still spread, but it will have to work that much harder to extend its reach."

"'You may have to fight a battle more than once to win it.' Thatcher, English," the middle figure proclaimed.

An optimist by nature, the youngest shook off her fears. "I'm ready. Count me in—whatever is needed, I'm here. To the edge of the universe and back. What do we do next?"

"Now we must go where we are needed and find those who are suffering to offer what help we can," the invisible being declared, her words reverberating in the air.

"'Heroes are made in the hour of defeat. Success is, therefore, well described as a series of glorious defeats.' Ghandi, Indian."

"Indeed," the oldest said. "Where there is strife we will find the bravest, kindest souls to join our fight against the IT's evil."

As one, the three rose into the sky, bursting out

of the atmosphere to hover in the infinite reaches of space. With a last glance at the dark orb, which had begun to slowly, achingly spin on its axis, the three beings zoomed away.

A pure note of despair soared out into the void and latched on to their souls. There.

In an instant, they folded through space to arrive in a spiral galaxy flooded with stars. The mournful sound tugged them down, past clusters of light and meteor fields to a solar system with but one life-sustaining planet.

Blue oceans, broken by green landmasses, covered the surface, but there was a murky haze hovering over it all.

"The IT is already here!" the youngest cried out in dismay.

"'Hope is being able to see that there is light despite all of the darkness.' Tutu, South African."

"She is right. There is always hope," the oldest soothed. "Now, let's find the warriors who will take up our cause."

Chapter Two
Meg Murry (Age Ten)

Headstrong and independent, Meg Murry is endlessly curious. She takes full advantage of being the daughter of two scientists and is always ready with an observation and a question (or two).

A clear sky unfolded before Meg Murry as she peered through the telescope in her attic bedroom. She knew she should go to sleep; her two-year-old brother would be up early the next day, weekend or not, but she couldn't resist completing one more star chart.

"Four degrees southeast . . ." Meg carefully marked another star on her paper, the pencil making a soft scraping noise.

She pushed her glasses back up on her nose

and turned the dial on the telescope, focusing it on a more distant star, then calculated its placement compared with the last. Just as she was about to lift her head, something burst into the frame.

"What on earth?" Meg cried, grasping the telescope with both hands to follow the object.

The bright light arced across the sky and was gone in a flash, just as quickly as it had appeared.

Meg bolted upright, her eyes filled with excitement. Eager to share her news, she scrambled away from the window and padded down the stairs, her fuzzy lavender slippers making no sound. On the ground floor, her mother's voice made her pause at the edge of the band of warm light spilling from the kitchen.

"He's so quiet, though," Dr. Kate Murry was saying. "Most of the other toddlers in the playgroup are at least saying *mama* and *dada* by now, and many even have full sentences."

They were talking about Charles Wallace, Meg's adopted younger brother.

"I don't think there's cause for concern yet," Dr. Alex Murry replied. "Remember, the doctor said every child develops on his own timeline. From the way he watches everything, it's clear he's taking it all in. He'll talk when he's ready. Besides"—a coffee cup thunked down on their wooden butcher block—"he makes his desires known quite clearly."

Meg could hear her father chuckling. It was true; Charles Wallace had a way of gazing at someone intently and then pointedly shifting his eyes to whatever he wanted, whether it was a box of animal crackers or the abacus on the top shelf.

"Yes, well. I was thinking," Meg's mother continued, "maybe next week we should set up an appointment with a speech therapist. Just in case there's something we should be doing to encourage him further. Some tools to use."

"If you'd like," Meg's father agreed affably. "Although I still don't think it's time to hit the panic button."

"I've been meaning to call, but I've been so absorbed in the presentation—"

"Did you look over the paragraph I added?" Meg's father interrupted her excitedly.

"I did. Alex, you have to remember our audience here. The scientists at NASA are not used to quantifying something as abstract as love. They're going to have trouble swallowing that it's the key to bypassing the four dimensions."

Meg eased into the hallway, poking her head around the doorframe but staying low. Her parents had been poring over their research and practicing their NASA talk for months, and the following night it would finally happen. While Meg didn't fully understand all the ins and outs and the quantum physics behind it, she knew her parents had made a breakthrough discovery. Something called a tesseract would allow people to travel *through* time *and* space in just *the blink of an eye*, without needing a rocket ship. How cool was that?

Her mother's eyes were crinkled in worry as she leaned against the sink.

"But we have the math to back it up!" Meg's father exclaimed, gesturing wildly with his hands. "They'll have to believe us."

Kate laid her hand on his arm, his skin looking paler against her light-brown fingers. "And they will, love, but we have to ease them into it." She picked up a piece of paper from the counter and pulled a red pen from the drawer. "Let's just move that section to later, after we've shown them the wavelength graph."

His shoulders slumping, Meg's father sighed. "Yeah, you're right." His eyes sparkled as he glanced up at his wife. "As always. Have I told you today how lucky I am you married me?"

A smile lit up her face and she leaned over to kiss him. "No, but feel free to show your appreciation by delivering a cup of cocoa to me in ten minutes."

She turned toward their lab, but caught sight of Meg in the doorway.

"Meg!" she said in surprise. "What are you doing up? It's almost eleven."

"I saw a shooting star, Mommy! Daddy! From my room." Meg bounced lightly on her toes, her curly hair flopping along with an energy all its own.

"You mean a meteoroid, Meg-a-nova," her father said, his blue eyes twinkling as he walked over and gave her a hug. "That's great."

"Yes, yes, a meteoroid." Meg rolled her eyes at him. "But shooting star *sounds* cooler."

"You don't need to sound cool to be cool," her mother jumped in, unable to resist. "It's what's inside that counts."

"Mo-o-o-om, I just mean it sounds more, I don't know, poetic."

Kate laughed at the dreamy look on her daughter's face. "Regardless, you should be in bed, my little astronomer."

"I'll take her up," Alex said. "Up, up, up, and away!" He swooped her up, even though at ten she was almost up to his shoulders.

"Eee!" Meg squealed in delight, her father's arms locked securely around her as he carried her up the stairs to the attic.

The lamp in the corner of Meg's room cast a warm glow as they ascended the last creaking step and crossed into her personal oasis. She'd been so excited when her parents agreed to let her move up there a year before and decorate it however she liked. The walls were painted in shades of light purple and her bed was tucked directly next to the main window, her telescope squeezed in at the head. Her homework for Monday was laid out neatly on her desk, next to her pencil case.

Her father lowered her to the floor as he crossed onto the plush rug surrounding her bed. Meg climbed in as he moved to the telescope and shifted it to the far wall.

"Let's tuck this away for the night, shall we? No more stargazing. It's time to sleep," he said, a faux-stern frown on his face.

Meg smiled in answer and pulled the covers over her legs.

"Sweet dreams," he said, bending to kiss her forehead.

"Daddy?" Meg's voice wavered. She cast her eyes down and fidgeted with a loose thread on her coverlet.

"Yes, my love?" He sank onto the mattress next to her.

"If you figure out how to travel through that tessa-thingy—"

"A tesseract. Yes?"

"Are you going to go away?"

Alex swept Meg into a hug, his beard tickling her forehead.

"Oh, my dear Meg-a-nova," he said. "No matter where I go or when, I will always come back to you."

He peppered her face with kisses until she squirmed away, giggling. Then, somberly, he sat back and studied her.

"You, your mom, and Charles Wallace mean the world to me," he told her. "Sometimes people have to go somewhere far away for a while, but no matter if I'm downstairs, across town, or on the other side of the planet, every part of me will still love you. Never doubt that."

He reached over and grabbed a piece of folded paper from the trunk that served as her bedside table.

"Remember what I told you when I gave you this," he said.

Meg remembered. He'd given her the enfolder just before they brought Charles Wallace home to live with them. As he turned one edge down, she could see a flash of color; two more sections unfolded and a hexagonal shape lay in his palm. In the center, where the three creased sections met, a red-and-yellow heart shone, its bright colors nearly filling the paper.

"Now you see it," her father continued. He took the paper and rearranged it, folding edges over and in until the heart disappeared. "Now it's not visible, but that doesn't mean it's gone. It's just enfolded."

"Not gone, just enfolded," Meg repeated.

He reversed his movements to unfurl the heart once again, then placed the heart in her hand.

"Always and forever, my dear, you have my heart. Love is always there, Meg, even when you can't see it."

Meg's own heart felt full of air, like helium had been pumped inside her and she'd float up to the ceiling any minute. She took the paper and copied his moves—folding and refolding and unfolding to hide and show the heart.

"Do you understand?" Her father gazed at her intently.

"Yes, Daddy." She beamed up at him.

"Excellent. Now get that math-whiz brain of yours some sleep in case we come home from NASA tomorrow with calculations that have stumped them."

She laughed and took her glasses off, setting them and the enfolder on the trunk next to the book she was reading.

"Good night, Daddy."

He ran his hand over her hair, then stooped to give her one more kiss.

"Good night, Meg. I'll see you in the morning."

Secure in his love for her, Meg had no trouble falling asleep—visions of where that meteoroid could have been going and where it had come from shooting through her head.

Chapter three

The Disappearance of Dr. Alex Murry

Dr. Alex Murry always encourages his daughter's exploration and curiosity. His sudden disappearance while trying to unlock part of the hidden structure of the universe has a powerful and instant effect on those closest to him.

Bright sunlight streamed through the window, nudging under Meg's eyelids. As she rolled away, snuggling determinedly into her pillow, she heard a crinkling sound and her fingers brushed against an object in her bed. Blinking awake, Meg spotted the enfolder next to her head.

Without her glasses, the heart looked a little

blurry, but the bold color was unforgettable. She smiled. The night before, she'd fallen asleep studying it, and she was almost ready to fashion her own. She'd been thinking she'd make one for Veronica to take to camp that summer, so she'd have something to remind her that far away, her best friend waited for her, no matter what drama she went through in the cabins.

Clink, clank. Muted noises from the kitchen drifted up to her room.

Fumbling for her glasses, Meg tumbled out of bed and headed for the stairs. At the bottom, she found her mother stirring the batter for pancakes, as usual. Also as usual, Charles Wallace was parked in his high chair, coloring far outside the lines of a picture. As Meg got closer, she had to admit—again—that Charles Wallace's additions made it more beautiful than if he'd stopped at the edges, the colors springing forth in exuberant spirals.

It was then that Meg noticed something amiss in the scene.

She scanned the kitchen again. It was a Sunday. Her father was always up before her and at the table with the paper, a red pen in hand as he whizzed through the crossword puzzle. But not that day.

"Um, where's Dad?" Meg asked, slipping into her own spot at the table.

"Hmm? What?" Meg's mother answered, a bit *too* breezily.

Peering closer, Meg realized her mother must have been mixing the pancake batter for ten minutes. It was more liquid than she'd ever seen it, the usual banana lumps mashed into oblivion. Her mom's eyes were dazed, but not in her *I haven't had coffee yet* way. This was different. There was an anxious turn to her lips and her hands were clutched around the bowl and spoon as though they were a life preserver keeping her afloat.

"Mom, are you okay?"

With a quick shake, her mom turned to her, her face strangely bright. "Of course I'm okay, sweetie. Just . . . I was up early, that's all."

Meg glanced at Charles Wallace to find his gaze locked on her, but he shook his head solemnly, as if to say he hadn't woken their mom up.

"Okaaay. So where's Dad?"

Meg's mom hesitated, a wave of unidentifiable emotions flickering over her features.

"I'm not sure. He wasn't here when I got up." She turned her back and began scooping batter onto the griddle. "Maybe he went to the store. Or maybe he got called in for a consultation."

Meg couldn't help arching an eyebrow at that. All week long, her father had been in a funk, swinging between self-recriminations for having "blown" her parents' presentation to NASA and outrage that the scientific community hadn't bothered to seriously consider the possibilities of their data. Her mom had shut off the news any time it came on, but the media's delight in the real-life nutty professor who claimed all people needed to do to travel through space was feel love . . . well, it had been unavoidable.

Any time he noticed it, her father had waved it off, uncaring what the masses thought; so Meg didn't mind, either, not even when the kids at school teased her about it. She knew how brilliant her parents were, and she wasn't going to let some small-minded people deter her faith in them.

Besides, if they could have seen what she had—the bold march of numbers up and down the page, zigzagging lines of vibration charted like a field of flowers dancing in the wind, the columns of color-coded data—then they'd have understood that her parents' work was beautiful, not some crackpot theory.

Nevertheless, it seemed unlikely that any institution would be seeking out her dad's help at this particular moment in time. Also, it was weird that he hadn't left a note or called or something.

A crayon plopped onto the floor from Charles Wallace's tray. Meg looked up to meet his earnest eyes, full of confidence in her. He glanced down to the floor, then back up at her, a wide smile filling his face.

With a laugh, Meg got up and retrieved his crayon for him. "There you go. No more runaway blue for you."

Meg's mom slid two pancakes onto her plate as Meg sat back down.

"Thank you, Mom," Meg said sweetly. She didn't comment on how flat they were.

Her mom smiled distractedly, then cleared off Charles Wallace's tray so he could eat, too. She barely settled in her chair, popping up to get an orange from the bowl or ladling more pancakes onto the griddle.

As they cleared the breakfast dishes, Meg eyed the stack of pancakes set aside for her dad, who still hadn't returned or called. She hoped he'd be home in time for Charles Wallace's nap that afternoon. He'd promised to take her to the park for some one-on-one court time, and she wanted his input on how to start the enfolder for Veronica.

But her dad wasn't home by naptime. Or dinnertime. Meg's mom had a harder and harder time hiding her anxiety as the day wore on. Meg felt her chest tightening in response.

When her mom tucked her in that night, Meg couldn't hold it in any longer.

"Mom, where's Dad?"

Her mom brushed her cheek with gentle fingers and met her gaze. "He'll be back as soon as he can," she said reassuringly. "Don't worry that brilliant brain of yours." She tapped Meg's nose and smiled at her. "Good night, Meglet."

Meg wiggled deeper into her mattress.

"Good night, Mom. I love you."

"I love you, too," her mom said from the door.

Dr. Alex Murry wasn't home the next morning, or the one after that. After two weeks of waiting and wondering, Meg was a ball of frayed nerves. How could he not let them know where he was? Why hadn't he come home yet?

"It's just not like him," she told Veronica.

They were at the park, sitting on the swings. Meg

scraped her feet through the gravel underneath her, feeling torn apart.

"He always checks in," Meg continued. "Even when he's at a conference, he'll go online with us every night to wish us sweet dreams and tell us he's looking forward to coming home." She thought about his disheveled hair, which would stand up after he'd run his hand through it, and even though he could see that on his own screen, he'd be so intent on them he wouldn't bother to tame it.

Meg blinked back tears and looked over at her friend.

Veronica's head was bowed, her smooth brown hair falling like a veil over her face. She'd been trying to coax Meg out for days, but now that they were there, she'd gone strangely silent. At least the weather was considerate enough to match Meg's mood, the gray clouds overhead blocking out the sun.

Finally, Veronica looked up, her mouth pursed in a frown.

"What if," she said, "he doesn't want to come home this time?"

The words were like a slap. Meg's whole body recoiled and her mouth dropped open in shock.

"Excuse me?" she asked.

Veronica had the decency to blush, but she pressed on. "What if he wants to start over somewhere else? Someplace nobody knows him or will make fun of him. My mom says sometimes people go looking for a fresh start. Maybe he wasn't happy here anymore. Or maybe he met somebody else."

Meg launched herself to her feet and spun to face Veronica head-on.

"You take that back, Veronica Kiley," she spat. "You know how much my dad loves us."

"Calm down, Meg," Veronica said. "I'm just saying what everyone else is: people change."

A fire burned in Meg's belly and rose up her chest, consuming all the sadness as it went.

"My dad is coming back," she snapped.

"You don't know that," Veronica said softly,

reaching out her hand. "Meg, I know this is hard to hear, but what if he's not?"

Meg reeled back, jerking away from Veronica's hand. She shook her head fiercely. "It's not true. He has to. He has to!" Her eyes locked on Veronica, her friend's perfectly brushed hair and bright pink shirt annoying her beyond reason.

"My dad loves us," she repeated loudly, clutching at the locket he'd given her. "He'd never leave us! You're an idiot for believing that. A stupid, sheep-following, blithering idiot, and your mom is, too," she exploded.

Veronica's expression hardened.

"You think you're above everyone else," Veronica spat out, her white teeth flashing in a sneer. "You're not. You're not special. And it's not like you'd be the first family a parent walked out on." Her chin ticked up defiantly.

Meg stiffened, her fiery anger suddenly turning icy.

"He didn't walk out on us," she hissed.

"Oh, really? Then where is he?" Veronica challenged.

"If you don't take it back right now, we are no longer friends." Meg held Veronica's gaze, deadly serious.

Veronica's mouth dropped open, and then she snapped it shut and stood up, the extra two inches she had on Meg obnoxiously seeming like a foot.

"First you take back saying my mom and I are idiots," she said, crossing her arms over her chest.

Meg glared at her. "No. You first." She crossed her arms, as well, her mouth settling into a grim line.

The two girls faced off in silence, their hearts both swollen with pride. In the distance, a trio of runners chugged past and a squirrel dove into the bushes. Down the street, the smell of rising dough wafted from the pizza parlor.

"Fine, then," Meg said after two minutes of waiting. "Consider our friendship null and void. You and your judgmental self are not welcome in my life anymore."

"What? Are you serious?" Veronica's eyebrows arched and she shook her head slightly, like she couldn't believe Meg was being so unreasonable.

But after lashing out, Meg's anger was starting to dissipate, and her pain came flooding back. Veronica's betrayal landed on top of the already giant pile of grief she was carrying around.

Before Veronica could say anything else, Meg whirled away and stomped across the playground, tears dribbling down her cheeks.

As she tore through the exit, she bumped someone with her shoulder.

"Whoa, sorry," a boy said.

Meg glanced up to see Calvin O'Keefe standing there, rubbing his own shoulder, a tentative smile on his lips. An internal groan shuddered through Meg. Of *course* she'd run into the cutest, most popular boy at school when her face was a runny mess. His expression changed when he saw her tears.

"Are you okay?" he asked. She saw him realize she was the girl whose father had been in the news only to then mysteriously vanish without a trace. She could see him registering all that, the information clicking in to form a picture. His eyes started to fill with pity.

She couldn't handle that. Not now. That might break her open.

"I'm fine," she said, brushing past him. "Sorry about your shoulder."

Then she was running down the sidewalk, the storefronts and houses a blur as she pelted past. By the time she got home, it felt like a giant was squeezing her chest, but it wasn't from the physical strain.

She pushed open the side gate and stumbled into the backyard, finally giving in to the crushing sadness. Kneeling in the too-long grass—her dad was the one who usually cut it—sobs racked her body, strange, inhuman noises she'd never made before.

Where was he?

When would he be back?

What if he'd been hurt? Or worse?

How could he leave them like this?

Creak. Meg heard the back door open. Soft footsteps, too light to be her mom's, padded down the porch to her side.

A small hand rested on her knee and Charles Wallace ducked his head to peer into her face, his gaze curious at first, then concerned. He was so young, so innocent. He didn't know what it all meant, that their dad was missing.

Meg tried to control her breathing, not wanting to scare him. She drew him onto her lap, wrapping her arms around the comforting weight of his body. Slowly, she rocked him back and forth, Charles Wallace waiting patiently until she calmed down.

Then he pulled something from his pocket and held it up to her.

Meg laughed and brushed away the remnants of her tears.

Lying in his little hand was a tiny yellow dandelion. He presented the weed to her like it was the most beautiful thing he'd ever seen. She felt another wave of sadness cresting—weeds were her dad's nemesis—but she tamped it down for Charles Wallace's sake.

"That's amazing, Charles Wallace," she said. "You're amazing and loved. Never forget that." She gave him one more fierce squeeze, then stood up and set him on the porch.

Inside the house, she could hear her mother on the phone. Gripping Charles Wallace's hand, Meg led the way indoors. Unlike its usual pristine state, the kitchen was in disarray—dirty pots and discarded vegetable peels covered the counter. Something was simmering on the stove—from the smell, it was some kind of stew.

Meg settled Charles Wallace in his chair with his crayons and set about clearing the counter. She couldn't do anything about the mess in her heart, but she felt a strange satisfaction in scrubbing the grime away from the pans and wiping the counter clean.

When her mother came in and saw her drying

the last of the dishes, her face broke into an expression of gratitude. Meg swore right then and there she'd do everything she could to help keep their family running, despite the hole in the middle.

She owed it to her mom and Charles Wallace, and to her father, wherever he was. They were the only ones who mattered now.

Meg Murry (Age Fourteen)

Middle school isn't easy for anyone, but Meg Murry has had a harder time than most. Not only is her father missing, but no one on Earth has had the chance to understand why or how he went missing, especially Meg. Her classmates and teachers are the first to notice the cracks beginning to show.

Even through the closed door of Principal Jenkins's office, Meg could hear the raised voice of Tristan's dad. She slumped down farther in her chair, doing her best to avoid the school secretary's stern gaze, but from the way Mr. Armand was stamping documents it was clear he was trying to send her a message. She was in trouble, big trouble. Again.

The door cracked open and Tristan's parents emptied into the outer office, their son planted between them. His dad had his hand on Tristan's shoulder, and he quickly steered him past Meg. A pang twisted Meg's heart. Tristan's dad was there, protecting him, guiding him. Lucky jerk.

She clenched her fist and stole a glance at Tristan. He was still cradling the ice pack against his cheek. His gaze darted over to hers and his mouth screwed into a tight frown when he saw her. Then he scuttled from the room like he was afraid of her.

As if he were the victim. Meg rolled her eyes.

Hem, hem. Principal Jenkins cleared his throat from his doorway, his eyes fixed on her.

Oops. Meg tried to look repentant as he gestured her into his office. She eased into a seat in front of his wide desk, clutching her backpack on her lap like a shield.

"Margaret Murry," Principal Jenkins said, stretching out her name like a reprimand. He lowered himself into his desk chair and leaned back, his hands cupped behind his head. "What am I going to do with you?"

"Um, tell me I've got a chance at a boxing career?"

The principal dropped his hands to his desk and sat up straight, his expression serious.

"This is no time for joking, young lady. You struck a fellow student."

"He swung first," Meg mumbled defiantly.

Not that anyone was likely to back her up, despite the small gathering of kids who'd been on the playground. Meg was an outcast, so nobody would take her side against star baseball player Tristan. But he *had* started it. He'd been calling her a dumb loser and making fun of her for wearing pants with holes in the knees. She'd told him she couldn't care less what he thought—that he was an inconsequential speck in her life. She doubted he knew what *inconsequential* meant, but his ears had flamed up nevertheless and she'd seen his arm pull back.

She'd danced backward as his hand went sailing past, throwing him off-balance. All she'd done was shove him away from her, but his face had hit the dirt at an angle, leaving him with a shiner. Tristan and his friends had scurried back to the school, calling her names over their shoulders. Ms. Langley had been on duty, and their cries had sent her stalking over to haul Meg into the office.

What was she supposed to do? Let him punch her? Oh, sure, her mom would have said to use words and walk away, but sometimes Meg felt this stubborn streak that forced her to stand still and face down the bullies.

Principal Jenkins was staring at her expectantly and Meg realized she'd tuned him out.

She shifted uncomfortably.

He sighed and shook his head.

"Meg, you need to stop lashing out at everybody. Look, I know you've got some tough circumstances at home—"

"We're fine," Meg said, cutting him off. She didn't want him poking and prodding in her family life.

"Well, I can't say I agree with you there, or you'd not be acting out like this. How many other kids do you see coming to my office on a regular basis?"

He didn't really expect an answer, so Meg gazed at the bulletin board on his wall instead. It was plastered with photos of smiling kids and thank-you cards from families grateful for the stellar education he provided. She snorted to herself. Like Principal Jenkins would know what a derivative was if it leapt off the page at him. Not that Meg's teachers were much better. Ms. Glotzer was always after her to show her work, as though it were impossible for her to just *get* math. Forget about the other subjects, where they just sighed at her answers.

"You're going to have to apologize, and I'm afraid you'll be in detention for the rest of the day."

That was fine with Meg; she didn't mind missing class. Fewer chances for people to snicker behind her back and lob paper at her.

"I've got a call in to your mother, too," Principal

Jenkins said, opening a drawer to pull out a notepad.

Meg winced. The last thing her mom needed was to be worrying about Meg.

"Can't we just . . ." Meg trailed off as Principal Jenkins shot her an *I don't think so* look. "Okay," she mumbled. "Can I go now?"

"Meg, we all just want what's best for you. You know that, right?" He folded his hands, the clunky gold ring on his finger catching the light. "Let us help you. If the other kids are giving you a hard time for some reason—"

Looking away, Meg glared at the dated carpet. He had no idea, no clue what it was like. The next day would mark four years since her dad had disappeared in a puff of smoke. Well, not literally a puff of smoke, or they'd have more clues than they did now.

Every day that passed was a fresh morning of grief, afternoon of bitterness, and evening of despair as another sliver of hope broke off and drifted away on the river of time.

Still, her mother maintained he'd be back; they just had to keep faith in him. Meg didn't know how her mom managed to never get mad that he was gone—not even when she was frantically packing their lunches as she tapped out a work e-mail on her phone and simultaneously took stock of what was running low in their pantry. The answer: usually everything. Charles Wallace ate his weight in crackers, animal and otherwise, and her mom usually put off shopping until the last possible minute.

But her mother's optimism never cracked, not even when she couldn't afford after-school art lessons for Charles Wallace or had to take gigs writing grants for other researchers to supplement her stipend. At times like that, Meg would opt not to ask her mom to check her English homework. And when she needed a new outfit, she'd stop by the thrift store, choking back envy when she saw Veronica and her mom hauling in ten shopping bags' worth of clothes from their car.

Who really cared what Meg wore anyway?

"Just . . . remember you can always make an appointment with Mr. Malone."

Meg blinked, her eyes refocusing on the dull gray floor. She knew Principal Jenkins meant well, but a session with the guidance counselor was not going to solve her problems.

She looked up to meet his gaze and saw the tight smile on his face.

"Thank you, Mr. Jenkins," she said, trying to muster a smile of her own.

He waved her out, and Meg bolted down the hall to the in-school detention room. She plunked herself in a chair by the window and gazed out at the palm trees, wishing with all her might that she could be one of the birds swooping between perches, carefree and immune to middle school drama.

Veronica Kiley

*The most dangerous aspect of the Darkness is how
easily it seeps into the lives of all living things. When
people feel weak or threatened, they lash out at those
around them, fracturing friendships and breaking
hearts. And since Darkness creates more Darkness, the
people who are hurt will reach out and hurt others.*

The hallways were abuzz with the usual morning chatter, everyone cramming in gossip with their friends before the teachers hustled them into the classrooms.

Veronica Kiley stood in the center of her circle, where Lorna McGuire and Adriana Morales were feasting on the update on Tristan's injury.

"How could she ruin such a gorgeous face?" Lorna asked. "Doesn't she know it's a crime against beauty?"

"I kind of think it makes him look more handsome." Adriana giggled.

Veronica suppressed an eye roll, wishing her friends didn't sound so ridiculous. "He's still no match for Calvin," she said instead.

"Of course not," they squealed.

Veronica spotted Elle Blumenthal sauntering down the hall. She stopped by a locker and taped a note on it. Veronica's eyebrows shot up. Was that Calvin's locker? No, it was the next one over. Meg's. She felt an uncomfortable wriggle in her stomach.

Elle joined them, a triumphant smirk on her face.

"What did you do?" Veronica asked, keeping her tone light.

"Oh, I just left Meg a little message—wouldn't want her to think we forgot the anniversary." Elle and the others snickered.

Veronica forced a small smile. Meg arrived, her curly hair springing around her face in an adorably unfussy way, red flannel shirt flapping open over her plain gray T-shirt and jeans. Veronica secretly wished she could pull off a look like that—low-key and down-to-earth. But whenever she tried, she lost her nerve, worrying her hair would end up frizzing and she'd look like a bum instead of casually chic.

Meg's expression froze when she found the note. That something in Veronica's stomach twitched again, but she stamped it down. Meg was the one who had walked away, choosing to toss out years of friendship. It wasn't Veronica's fault she was a loner. If Meg had reached out just once, one little "hi," maybe things would be different. But she'd turned her nose up every time Veronica tried to smile at her those first months after their fight, and Veronica got sick of trying. There were plenty of girls who actually wanted to be her friend, so why bother with someone who hated her?

Meg yanked her locker door open and slammed it shut without even taking anything out. Calvin had come up next to her, but she totally ignored him. Veronica could see Calvin's confusion as Meg stomped off.

Why couldn't she be just a little bit nice?

As she went by, Meg's eyes cut to Veronica, a look of withering disgust painted on her face.

Elle, Lorna, and Adriana collapsed into hysterical giggles after Meg passed, and Veronica pretended to join in. If her friends knew how much Meg's glare had hurt her, they'd never understand.

When she saw Meg later in the locker room before gym, Veronica hesitated. Should she say something?

Meg glanced up, spotted her old friend, and just . . . rolled her eyes.

Fine, Veronica thought. *I'm better off without you anyway.*

Ten minutes later, Coach Stewart had assigned them to the same basketball team for the period.

Veronica suppressed a sigh. Meg was hopeless at sports.

Sure enough, during warm-up drills, she fumbled the ball. Was it so hard to just grab hold of it? Meg was excellent at holding grudges; Veronica would have thought a rubber ball wouldn't be that much of a challenge. Coach whistled the start of a five-on-five game.

Adriana bounced the ball to Veronica, and she dribbled it down the line. Her hair swished back and forth in its ponytail, brushing her shoulders. Veronica wouldn't admit it, since the cool girls tended to cheer from the sidelines rather than compete, but she really enjoyed being on the court. She loved the feel of her fingers on the ball, controlling its movement, lining up for a shot, and then hearing the *swoosh* as the ball dropped through the basket— part practice, part natural ability.

Blocked by an opponent, she lobbed it back to her friend. Adriana pivoted and saw Meg open.

Veronica started to object, but it was too late. Adriana had already let the ball go.

"Get it, Meg! Get it!" Veronica cried.

Meg startled—clearly her mind had been elsewhere—and stumbled toward the ball. It rebounded off her elbow somehow—her elbow!—and skidded between her feet.

She tumbled to the ground, trapping the ball under her skinny legs.

"Seriously?" Veronica groaned. "Come on!"

Shaking her head, Veronica tried to rally the team. She raced after the ball, now in Cassidy Lang's possession, and managed to steal it back. *Yes!*

Veronica pounded down the court, eyes fixed on the basket. A school-issued purple gym shirt streaked into her periphery and she spun, dodging around Sybil Patterson, who was lunging for the ball.

Not today, thought Veronica gleefully.

The only one between her and the hoop now was Meg, who was staring off at the track.

"Coming through!" Veronica called.

But bizarrely, as Meg registered her words, she moved *toward* her, not away. Veronica didn't have time to adjust.

Bam!

The two girls collided, Meg's gangly limbs smacking Veronica in the face.

"Ow! Get out of the way! You're such a waste of space!" Veronica shoved Meg off, but the damage was done.

Thump, thump, thump. The ball bounced away, only to be scooped up by a smirking Sybil.

Veronica gritted her teeth and charged after Sybil as she broke for the other side. Adriana tried to stop her, but Sybil passed it to Cassidy, who had been waiting under the hoop. Veronica's shoulders itched in irritation as Cassidy scored.

It wasn't fair. Her team was a player short. No, worse than that, Meg was a liability. She shot a glare at Meg, who was, again, staring off at the field. Wait, was she watching Calvin?

Veronica snorted. Like Meg would have a chance with him. Even the nicest kid in the school wouldn't want to put up with her snooty attitude.

Someone yelled out from the elementary school yard above them. It was Meg's younger brother, Charles Wallace.

He was clinging to the chain-link fence and shouting down to his sister.

"You may be a mess," he called—Veronica couldn't agree more—"but you have more potential than anyone here!"

Um, no, Veronica thought. *Don't puff her up more!*

Wincing, Meg looked around in a panic.

"Trust me!" Charles Wallace continued, oblivious to how weird he sounded. "Mommy was awkward and funny-looking at your age, too, and look at her now. She's beautiful!"

Veronica snickered at the mortified look on Meg's face.

"Looks like crazy runs in the family," Veronica

taunted, ignoring the part of her that wished she had a brother who liked her that much. Still, she wouldn't want him announcing it to the world.

Adriana bounced the ball toward them and, miracle of miracles, Meg reached out and grabbed it.

Now she catches it, Veronica thought. *Where was that move ten minutes ago?*

"What did you say?" Meg's eyes were steely as she snapped at Veronica.

An ugly feeling warped Veronica's heart. Her ex-best friend was staring at her like *she* was the villain. Like she was the one who'd stabbed Meg in the heart.

Meg had no right. She was the one who had turned her back on Veronica, who refused to answer the door when she came to make up, who stuck her nose up at Veronica at school, who made snide comments about her and her friends. Meg only cared about herself. She hadn't cared when Veronica's dog died two years before, hit by a car in front of their houses. Or when Veronica had been humiliated in the school presidential election the previous year. She definitely hadn't voted for her. The ugliness bubbled up Veronica's throat and popped out.

"I can see why your dad left."

Inside, the part of her that still cared about her former friend churned in guilt as soon as the words dropped from her lips. It was a low blow. But before she could retract it or apologize, Meg hurled the basketball at her.

A blur of neon orange slammed into her nose and forehead.

Veronica's hands flew up to her face. Her nose felt like it had been smashed flat—was that blood?— and her head was pounding as though a little elf were running around inside, swinging a sledge-hammer at her skull. She pulled one hand away.

Through blurry vision she saw bright scarlet staining her fingers.

Hands were suddenly all around her, supporting her back and elbows.

"Oh my god, I can't believe she did that!" Adriana squealed.

"Are you okay?" Sybil's voice called from farther away.

"Let's get you to the nurse," Coach Stewart said. "Adriana, go with her."

As her friend, a true friend, wrapped her arm around Veronica and guided her off the blacktop, Veronica glanced back.

Coach Stewart, arms crossed, was rebuking Meg. But from the stubborn look on Meg's face, she didn't seem to regret it at all. Nevertheless, Veronica felt a surge of satisfaction when she spotted Calvin watching Meg. That was all the proof he needed of Meg's cruelty.

Wait, was he . . . smiling?

"Ewww!" Adriana squealed as blood dripped from Veronica's nose.

Whimpering, Veronica tipped her face back, losing sight of Meg and Calvin, and pinched the bridge of her nose to stem the flow. After years of mistreating Veronica, Meg had just added injury to insult. Veronica would corner Calvin later and fill him in on what a wretch Meg Murry was. Right now, she desperately needed a painkiller. And a tissue.

chapter six

Charles Wallace

Charles Wallace is many things—intelligent, caring, blunt, insightful—but more than anything, he has the ability to see the truth in those around him. This is one of the things his mother and sister, Meg, love most about him, even if it's also one of the things that can drive them up the wall.

Some people called Charles Wallace strange. Some people called him crazy. More generous folks said he marched to a beat only he could hear, and this last, at least, was true. The world spoke to him in a way it didn't seem to connect with others. Charles Wallace thought it was because nobody else bothered listening. But perhaps it had more to do with the fact that Charles Wallace was gifted with a unique mind that never stopped working.

Nobody knew who his birth parents were. All the adoption agency could tell the Murrys was that his blood type was O positive and he had been found wrapped in a flannel scarf on the steps of the library. Perhaps his birth mother had mistaken its columned entrance for a police station. The Murrys opened their hearts wide to him from the start, so Charles Wallace never longed to know more about his origins. Besides, he was too busy discovering his world.

When he was a baby, his thirst for new experiences had been undeniable; he had happily slurped up any food offered to him, from spicy curries to sweet desserts, and smiled biggest on walks, where he could take in novel surroundings and people. His adoptive parents had fretted over some developmental delays; he'd never babbled or tripped over words like other toddlers. But when he turned three, he began firing out complete, grammatically correct sentences with no hesitation, as though he'd simply been waiting to have a full command of the English language before choosing to communicate even the simplest request with it.

While other preschoolers zipped around the playground, chasing each other, Charles Wallace spent hours witnessing an ant traverse a sandy pit or lying in the grass, studying the trees overhead. Once he was in school, his teachers were perplexed at the maturity of his answers but tsked to themselves when he failed to make close friends. *If only his mother had more time to devote to his social development,* they'd mutter, despite how unfair it was to cast judgment on a single parent.

Even though he was odd, his classmates didn't ridicule him. They treated him like an unusual alien in their midst—one who made fascinating pronouncements that unnerved their teachers and who could be counted on to help search for lost objects on the playground.

Charles Wallace never hesitated to lend a hand, no matter who asked. When he did good deeds, a thrum of happiness tingled from the tips of his toes to the top of his head. Ripples of kindness flowed out from him, and although they were invisible to anyone else, Charles Wallace marveled at their mesmerizing colors. In tune as he was with the world around him, it did not surprise him when the universe came calling.

All day, the air around him had trembled with thrilling possibility, like a balloon had been rubbed on his hair and then passed over his skin so all the individual hairs stood up. Whispers of something *big* had come from the trees, and the bees in Ms. Gladwater's garden buzzed frenetically as he walked by them on the way home from school. Stomping along beside him, Meg hadn't even noticed.

Charles Wallace decided not to tell her yet. He wanted to discover the mystery on his own first.

"I'm going to take Fortinbras for a walk," he announced when they arrived home.

"Don't go too far," Meg warned, already opening the fridge to brainstorm dinner.

Clipping the leash on their black lab, Charles Wallace coughed noncommittally. He'd go as far as he needed.

Fortinbras's claws scraped over the sidewalk, the wizened dog unusually eager. Charles Wallace laughed.

"I'm coming, Fortinbras. No need to pull my arm off," he said.

Just a few blocks away from their house, the neighborhood shifted, signs of wear and tear cropping up. Storefronts were shuttered, and houses crowded together, many of them also covered in plywood. Usually, Charles Wallace soaked in the graffiti, admiring the bold colors and unique tags, but that day he scrambled past, sensing his destination ahead.

At the bottom step of a residence with an overgrown lawn and a darkened interior, Fortinbras stopped, his tongue lolling.

"Yup, this is the place," Charles Wallace agreed. A sparking zing like bubbly soda up his nose popped along his skin.

Fearlessly, Charles Wallace climbed the stairs to the sagging porch, Fortinbras ambling beside him.

At the door, Charles Wallace knocked politely, even though the presence inside was fiercely inviting him in with unspoken energy.

Someone flung open the door.

"Hello!" A red-haired woman appeared, speaking in a bright voice. She was draped in a what looked like a flowing, comfortable white dress.

"Hello," Charles Wallace answered, cocking his head. Her hair was swept to one side of her head. As Charles Wallace looked closer, he saw her toes sticking out from the bottom of her dress, and realized that she was barefoot. He was more distracted by her presence, though. Her mind seemed endless, like he was gazing at an ocean with unknown depths, while most people he met had minds that were contained, like wells or ponds.

She couldn't be human. His heart thumped with excitement.

"Please, come in," she continued, beaming at him. "We've been expecting you."

Fortinbras shuffled past her into the house, giving her his seal of approval. As he went by, she reached out and ran her fingers over his fur, her eyes widening. She held her hand up in front of her, as though she were looking for evidence that she'd sprouted fur of her own.

"I've been expecting you, too," Charles Wallace said, knowing it to be true. For weeks he'd been antsy and sketching spirals of energy in his notepad. He'd known a change was coming soon.

The house was different from anything Charles Wallace had seen before. The inner rooms of the house were filled with books, from the floor to the ceiling. The overgrown lawn had worked its way inside the house, leaving branches and flower petals scattered across the books and furniture.

Snuggled on a square floor pillow seemingly designed for him, Fortinbras snorted happily. The woman was crouched next to him, giggling every time he breathed onto her face. She didn't exactly glow, but there were tiny lights dancing around her—like fireflies. Even though she felt familiar, Charles Wallace didn't know her name.

"I'm Charles Wallace," he offered.

"Oh!" She shot upright, clapping her hands. "Of course. Introductions. It's so hard to remember all the steps sometimes. We have no need of such formalities where I come from, so please forgive my mistake. I'm sure it won't be the only one I make. This is all still so new to me. You can call me Mrs. Whatsit."

"Hello, Mrs. Whatsit," he said, the name skipping into his ears. It was perfect for her.

"Come along, come along, you must meet the others," Mrs. Whatsit said, whisking him toward a beaded doorway.

Dozens of little balls tickled his arms as he followed her into a warm kitchen decorated with blown-glass lanterns and hanging plates from around the world.

Mrs. Whatsit swished over to a seated dark-haired woman, who peered at him curiously through the strangest pair of glasses he'd ever seen. They were a solid inch thick and cut like prisms, casting her brown eyes into dozens of smaller images. A saffron yellow tunic complemented her light-brown skin, and a ball of yarn rested in her lap as though she'd been untangling it. Like Mrs. Whatsit, she seemed to attract tiny sparks that filled the air around her.

"Charles Wallace, meet Mrs. Who." Mrs. Whatsit gestured to her companion. "Mrs. Who, here he is! What do you think?"

Reaching forward, Mrs. Who grasped his hands between her own and gazed up at him.

"'Let my soul smile through my heart and my

heart smile through my eyes, that I may scatter rich smiles in sad hearts.' Yogananda, Indian," Mrs. Who said.

Her welcoming smile buoyed his heart, like there was a hot-air balloon beneath it. He grinned in return.

"Words don't come naturally to us, you know. We communicate so much faster with thoughts. So Mrs. Who prefers to express herself with the sayings of others from your planet," Mrs. Whatsit explained.

As Charles Wallace gazed at them, the word *marvel* slid into his thoughts. They were both marvels, and that was exactly what he was doing—marveling at their impressive, expansive minds. He'd have to tell Meg his new word of the day, even if he couldn't tell her its inspiration. He wondered where the two women could be from.

"That's one of the reasons I was chosen, you know. My excellent verbosity. I'm quite the talker," Mrs. Whatsit prattled on, as Charles Wallace looked up for the first time and saw the interlocking tree branches across the ceiling.

"Excuse me," Charles Wallace began hesitantly. "Could you tell me where you're from?"

"Why, isn't that obvious? We're celestial beings. The three of us have come to Earth to answer a desperate summons and to find our newest champions in the most important war."

"'Three of us'?" Charles Wallace repeated.

"Mrs. Which, would you mind taking form for Charles Wallace?" Mrs. Whatsit's tone was extremely respectful.

"It would be my pleasure," a deep voice rumbled.

The air next to the counter shimmered and a translucent figure appeared. She was cloaked in a regal ball gown of pearly white, as though she were wreathed in clouds.

"You are as remarkable as we'd hoped," Mrs. Which said to Charles Wallace, gazing into his eyes.

She read the very corners of his soul in that moment and smiled at what she saw.

Charles Wallace stood up straighter. "You said something about a summons and a war?"

"Yes, from across the universe we heard the call—we were needed here," Mrs. Whatsit replied. "There is a darkness spreading. The IT has taken root on Earth, and we believe the best way to help may be to find your father." She beamed at him, as though it were perfectly natural to bring up his father. Most adults doggedly avoided the topic near him.

"My dad?" Charles Wallace couldn't truly remember his dad, who'd disappeared before his memories were fully formed, but he'd left an impression on Charles Wallace's brain—like a fingerprint in clay. He'd been a poet at heart, always looking for the beauty in the world. Charles Wallace liked to imagine long conversations with him about the benefits of untamed gardens over structured planting beds. But on the whole, Charles Wallace was content with his life. He knew Meg and his mom would be transformed by his dad's return, though, and he was curious what it would be like to have two parents.

"Yes," Mrs. Which chimed in. "He's a pioneer in science, and through enlightenment, the Darkness is often beaten back."

"'Education is the most powerful weapon which you can use to change the world.' Mandela, South African," Mrs. Who said with a nod.

"We'd like to help you get him back," Mrs. Whatsit continued.

"Really? You can do that?" His skin prickled. With his father home, his family would be whole.

"Not just us—we need you to guide our search. You see, we haven't been able to pinpoint his location yet," Mrs. Whatsit said. She popped another piece of cinnamon bun into her mouth.

Mrs. Who jumped in again. "'If I have ever made any valuable discoveries, it has been owing more to patient attention than to any other talent.' Newton, English."

"Yes, indeed!" Mrs. Whatsit exclaimed. She leaned down toward Charles Wallace. "Do you think you could bring us a photograph of him, by chance? It would help Mrs. Who focus her mind's eye on his location."

Charles Wallace nodded furiously. He'd give them anything they asked for and do whatever it took.

Mrs. Which's figure became more solid, and she laid a strong hand on his shoulder.

"I must warn you, Charles Wallace. If he's where we think he is, he's in terrible danger. As we said, a dark force has been overtaking the universe, and we fear it may have something to do with your father's disappearance. You will have to be brave. There are places you may need to go where we cannot follow."

"Of course, we don't expect you to rescue him on your own," Mrs. Whatsit interjected cheerfully. "You can pick the other warriors for the mission."

"My sister, Meg," Charles Wallace said immediately.

"Are you sure?" Mrs. Whatsit asked skeptically.

"I've only seen her one time myself, but she seems, well . . . troubled."

"I'm sure." Charles Wallace nodded. Meg might not be perfect, but she loved him and her father wholeheartedly. He needed her by his side.

"All right. But you may have your work cut out for you getting her ready. We don't have a lot of time." Mrs. Whatsit tapped her finger on her chin, her lips pursed. "You may want a third champion, too."

"I'll find one." Charles Wallace was confident.

"We have faith in you, my dear," Mrs. Which said.

Charles Wallace glanced out the window into the backyard, his mind already spinning with ideas and plans.

" 'The seat of knowledge is in the head; of wisdom, in the heart.' Hazlitt, English," Mrs. Who suggested kindly.

Charles Wallace nodded gravely. "I'll listen to my heart," he promised.

Looking at the three figures before him, he beamed with excitement. Yes, the dangers were great, the risks high, but he was ready. He'd bring home his father and help heal his family.

The IT

Just as Mrs. Whatsit, Mrs. Which, and Mrs. Who
are champions of the Light, there is a being that
is a manifestation and champion of the Darkness
throughout the universe. The force known only
as the IT resides on the planet Camazotz, but
the true danger comes from the IT's reach.

It's not bragging to say that I am the single greatest intellect in all the universe. It's simply a fact. I have traveled the length and breadth of space, and no being I have encountered is my equal.

It could make for a lonely existence, but I have devised a strategy whereby I have constant companionship, so there is no possibility of loneliness.

True, it is relatively difficult for my central form to engage in physical contact. I have evolved past a body and am best described as an intricate network that houses my conscience. To spell it out for the humans out there—I look like that most delicate and fearsome organ, the one you barely use: the brain. But touch is vastly overrated in many societies. The purest form of connection is mental, and there I excel. I am the best friend anyone could imagine.

You see, I can enter any mind, human or alien, and find what troubles it most. With my superior capability, I know how to soothe the most anguished soul. All you have to do is let me in, and I can ease your heartache, erase your worries, and remove all fear.

It has become my lifelong goal to help as many souls as possible. I wish to lift up the burdens of others and take them upon myself. Do not trouble yourself over the weight it places on me—I can handle it.

chapter seven

Why would I heap such responsibilities upon myself, you ask?

The answer is simple.

I wish to spread peace throughout the universe.

Wherever you find conflict, that is where some are stupidly trying to resist me—those who cling to their problems in the name of some hollow freedom. Poor misguided fools. If they would only surrender, they would discover the bliss that I can deliver.

Take Camazotz, for instance. Here, I have bestowed upon the people a harmonious society. No wars, battles, or even childish spats occur, because through me, everyone is joined together. No longer a crowd of individuals clamoring for *me, me, mine, me, me, mine,* they are content with an ordered, predictable life in which no one feels pain or hunger, cold or loneliness. I have stamped out jealousy and anger, vanquished misery and deceit. Where I reign, there is no regret for the past or fear of the future, for all under my benevolent guidance can rest easy knowing I will take care of everything. I ask only for what each person can provide to the whole, and in return, there is peace.

That seems reasonable, don't you think? Surely, safety is the most important thing. Freedom of thought is a trifling thing to exchange for a stable life.

Wouldn't you like to live free of stress, immune to pain and disease, as a part of something grand and noble?

All you have to do is let me help you. Many on Earth already have, you know. My presence there is growing every day. The process itself can be somewhat rocky—more conflicts often flare up at the start—but once I have won over the entire planet, life will flourish and the fighting will stop.

Yes, Earth is proving to have a more contentious population than I was expecting. But little by little, the ones I have already begun to influence will sway the balance.

There is no doubt: I will rise above and secure the planet's future.

Trust me.

Calvin O'Keefe

*Popular, charming, eager to please, and personable,
Calvin has a calm exterior that exists in defiance of
his upbringing, not because of it. A compassionate
force in his own right, Calvin helps Meg and Charles
Wallace in their search for their father not only out
of admiration for them both but also because he
has long dreamed of having a father like Dr. Murry
instead of being raised under Darkness's shadow.*

The rumble of the garage door opening vibrated through the walls to where Calvin sat in the dining room. He lowered his head, hoping his dad was in a good mood from work, and squinted at the math workbook on the hardwood table in front of him. He was saving his favorite subject, English, for last as a reward; first, though, he was dutifully struggling through math homework.

Why couldn't it be word problems? He was better at those. Assigning real-life objects and concepts like speed always seemed to make the numbers more tangible. But word problems had been left behind the year before, and eighth graders were expected to solve for an abstract like the letter X with no trouble.

A door slammed and the staccato clicking of leather-soled shoes approached down the hallway and paused in the entryway.

Calvin's shoulders tensed.

Pasting on a smile, he looked up. "Hi, Dad. How was work?"

His father's green eyes narrowed, the skin around them wrinkling in suspicion. His face was clean-shaven, and while his salt-and-pepper hair was styled in a casual wave, Calvin knew a cup of grease kept it stiffly in place.

"Productive, as it should be." His father's smooth

voice filled the room, bouncing off the empty walls. It always surprised Calvin how melodic his father's voice could be. If it matched his persona, it would be a gravelly bellow. Or piercing, like the sharpening of knives. "Not done with your schoolwork yet? What have you been doing all day?"

"I stayed late for that canned food drive I told you about," Calvin said, pressing the eraser of the pencil into his bottom lip.

"Stop that. It's a disgusting habit." His father reached out and snagged the pencil from him, then tossed it onto the table.

It clattered and rolled before tipping over the edge and plummeting to the floor.

"I thought I told you not to waste your time with that." Mr. O'Keefe crossed his arms, flattening his red tie against his chest. "Volunteer work only counts in high school, and you need to be the main organizer, not just the lowly help."

Not expecting or needing an answer, his dad turned and strode into the kitchen. He dropped his keys into a bowl with a jangle. The fridge door opened and closed with a thump, and then there was the hiss of air escaping from a bottle.

Calvin's father reappeared, sparkling water in hand. He glided around the table to the living room as Calvin shifted in his chair, wishing for the millionth time his parents would allow cushions. But no, that wouldn't match the decor.

"I put in a call to Brent Lumbach today. Should be no trouble getting you on the football team next fall. Of course, you need to bulk up first." His dad turned and eyed him, the late afternoon light silhouetting his head and shoulders against the window.

"Um, thanks, Dad," Calvin said, falling into his role.

His dad snorted and took a gulp of his drink. "You're going to have to be more aggressive, too, or the players—and I'm including your own teammates here—will chew you up."

Calvin nodded. He knew this speech well. He was too nice, too soft. He needed to be driven to win, keep his eyes on the prize. Great players didn't need to be liked, just respected. As his dad got to the part about not embarrassing him in front of the coaches and other dads, Calvin's eyes caught on the algebra equation before him. The *X* stared back at him tauntingly.

"Are you listening to me, Calvin?" His dad's voice was level, but an ominous undercurrent ran through the syllables.

Calvin snapped his gaze up to his dad, whose expression was smug. He had been pacing but was now still, like a tiger bunching its muscles before an attack.

Oh, no, Calvin thought.

"Yes, Dad—of course, Dad." Calvin kept his tone neutral. "I won't let you down."

"Ha!" His dad guffawed and plunked his drink down on the sleek marble fireplace, which was empty of any photos or baubles ("dust collectors," as his mother called them). "Too late for that. I don't know where you get your sniveling, spineless personality, because it's certainly not from me." His eyes bored into Calvin's and he pointed a finger at him. "If you don't get your act together, you will go nowhere in life. Everyone else will step on you on their way to the top, and you'll wind up squashed at the bottom. Is that what you want? To end up living in an alley with rats for company, picking through trash for food?"

Betrayal and disappointment sliced through Calvin. Why couldn't his dad ever picture him in a good way? Was he really that much of a mess? If he didn't get perfect grades, get into the best college, get the right job . . . would his parents truly abandon him?

Not trusting his voice, Calvin just shook his head in answer.

"Well, then stop worrying about what everyone else thinks and listen to me. You spend too much energy trying to make people like you. Life isn't a popularity contest. It's a game of skill, and the more ruthless you are, the further you'll go."

His pocket beeped. Calvin's dad pulled out his phone and checked the message.

"You've got to be kidding me. Can't anyone do their job right?" he barked at the screen. Glancing up at Calvin, he frowned. "I've got to take care of this. When I get back, I want your homework all done."

Calvin slumped in momentary relief as his father stalked to his home office, phone already pressed to his ear. With a deep sigh, Calvin bent and rescued the pencil from the floor. Straightening, he peered down at the page again.

Maybe if he squared both sides he'd figure out how to move X. . . .

As Calvin tackled the math, an odd pressure tugged at his chest. He rubbed his shirt unconsciously and bit his lip before remembering that was also a bad habit that showed weakness. Slowly, he cracked the mystery of X, but the pressure in his chest built until he couldn't ignore it anymore.

He knew what it was. It was the same nagging sense that had once led him to a puppy trapped in a drainage ditch, unable to scramble up its steep sides. After Calvin boosted it out, the puppy had licked his face all over, its tongue warm and sticky, its breath smelling faintly of chewed-up grass. He'd known what his parents would say, but he'd tried to bring it home anyway. Predictably, his mother had shrieked in alarm and his father had ordered, "Get that *thing* to a shelter. Now." Calvin had never felt as horrible as when he'd handed the puppy over, its trusting eyes saying it knew he'd come back for it soon. Even though it was a no-kill shelter—Calvin had researched it thoroughly—and he knew puppies had a higher chance of adoption, there were still times he worried about where it had wound up.

The tugging in his chest was now an insistent yank, like someone had lassoed his heart and lungs.

A roar emerged from his dad's office before his voice settled back into its usual cutting tirade. From the sounds of it, his dad would be tied up for a while.

Might as well investigate where his intuition

or the universe or whatever was tugging on him wanted him to go.

Shoving down a twinge of guilt, Calvin swept his workbooks and school supplies off the table and stuffed them into his backpack by the door. He could always stay up late to finish. It wasn't like his parents would expect him to hang out with them after dinner or anything.

As soon as he was outside, his muscles relaxed. It was impossible to feel stressed on such a gorgeous day, with a slight breeze softening the heat of the sun into a delicious warmth.

Whistling to himself, Calvin set off, letting the feeling lead him down the block. As the manicured lawns of his neighborhood gave way to a small strip of stores, he peered into the window of a comic book shop, wondering if they had the latest edition of his favorite graphic novel. Unfortunately, he'd left his wallet at home. Besides, the tugging was pulling him onward, beyond the store.

The houses on the other side were more neglected, as were the sidewalks—the slabs poking up unevenly. It was getting late and Calvin knew he should turn back, head for home, but that feeling in his chest wouldn't let him just yet.

A yard full of tinkling wind chimes made him pause and smile at the colorful garden spinners. Light bounced off one of the whirling metal arms, dancing over his face. It was a place full of joy, but it wasn't where he was supposed to be.

The sensation pulled him to the left, and he crossed the street and turned the corner to an abandoned-seeming stretch of houses with sagging porches. To his surprise, Meg Murry and her kid brother were standing on the sidewalk with an enormous black lab panting happily between them.

"Don't be like me," Meg was saying.

"What's wrong with being like you?" Calvin asked. Meg was one of the most intriguing kids at school. She didn't worry about what other people

thought of her. She just was who she was. But as the words popped out of his mouth, he felt the back of his neck heat up. "You've got a pretty good arm," he added quickly.

"What?" Meg asked, her eyebrows furrowed.

"Veronica—direct hit," Calvin explained, tossing an imaginary ball her way.

Meg shifted on her feet, her smile tight. He hoped he hadn't offended her by bringing it up.

A head of floppy brown hair appeared at his waist, cutting between him and Meg.

"Hi, I'm Charles Wallace," Meg's brother piped up. "You're Calvin, aren't you?"

"I am," Calvin replied. How did Charles Wallace know him? Did Meg talk about him at home?

"What are you doing here?" Meg asked. She didn't sound mad, just curious.

"I don't know," Calvin began. He glanced around again at the neighborhood. "I was doing my homework, and all of a sudden, I just felt like I had to come here." His gaze wandered back to Meg. She was staring at him. "Is that weird?"

"Mmm. Maybe a little," she answered, her nose wrinkling up in humor.

"You're here because I called you here with my mind," Charles Wallace explained. His voice and expression were deadly serious, no hint of humor in them.

Calvin felt more than saw Meg suck in her breath, as though bracing herself for Calvin's answer. She needn't have worried—he loved younger kids, had always wanted a sibling himself, and wished he had Charles Wallace's bright confidence.

"Really?" Calvin leaned down. "So you have superpowers," he whispered admiringly.

"Something like that." Charles Wallace shrugged. "And I really think we could use a guy like you. You're good at diplomacy."

"What do we need diplomacy for?" Meg asked, winding the dog's leash around her hand and then spooling it out again. The dog rolled its eyes up at her, as though telling her to hold still.

Charles Wallace gently shook his head. "The fact that you asked is exactly why we need it." He turned back to Calvin, his face a pool of earnestness. "What do you say, Calvin? Want to come with us?"

Calvin stood up and smiled happily at Meg. He had no idea where this was going, but it sounded like fun. The pressure in his chest had eased, so apparently the invisible force wanted him there, with them. "Why not?"

"Great!" Charles Wallace held out his hand and solemnly shook Calvin's as though they'd just agreed to undertake a wilderness expedition together. "Let's meet Mrs. Who."

With that mysterious statement, Charles Wallace skipped across the street. For the first time, he seemed like the little boy he was—hopping one stair at a time up the steps of an old house with boarded-up windows. Considering its condition, the house's only occupants should have been ghosts and mice.

"Charles Wallace, come down from there," Meg called sternly.

But Charles Wallace ignored her. He gave a quick knock on the door, and it swung inward.

Meg stalked to the edge of the sidewalk. "Do *not* go in there," she ordered.

Her brother beamed back at her as though she'd told him an amusement park lay inside, and slipped through the door.

"Argh." Meg gritted her teeth beside Calvin.

"Fearless little guy," he said.

"Unfortunately," she muttered. Tugging her dog to standing, she stomped across the street, pausing at the bottom step to loop the leash around the rail.

What an interesting family, Calvin thought as he followed her up the stairs. *I wonder who Mrs. Who could be.*

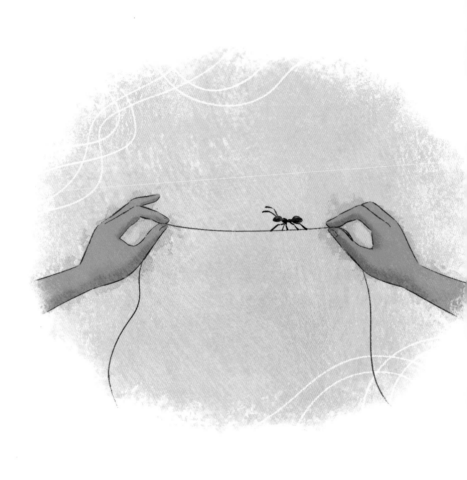

chapter nine
Tessering

*Despite all of humanity's grand achievements, as a
species we are only beginning to see our true place in
the universe. But where some are rendered helpless
by the crushing weight of the size and scope of the
universe, there are people like Drs. Alex and Kate Murry
who see only opportunity. In a breakthrough that has
the potential to change not only the lives of these two
physicists but of everyone on the planet Earth, the
husband-and-wife team discovered that the universe
is far more interconnected than anyone realized.*

Imagine you are standing on an invisible string
stretched over a gaping chasm. The shortest
way to get to the other side using the three
spatial dimensions—length, width, and height—
and the fourth dimension—time—would be to walk

across. Step by shaky step, you'd wobble over. But if there were a way for you to access a dimension *outside* the rules we know of time and space, then you could fold time up, as though looping the string to tug the two sides of the canyon together, and with just one step . . . arrive at your destination.

This is what a tesseract does. It wrinkles time so you can move instantaneously through time and space. But for it to work properly, you need to know just the right frequency and be in tune with who you are. Otherwise . . .

Earth slides underneath you, shaking with power. You stumble and steady yourself with feet wide. The vibrations build, juddering up your muscles until your teeth start to chatter and your eyesight quivers. It *must* be quivering. There can't really be ripples in everything around you—the house, the willow tree, the fence all getting hit by an invisible wave that rolls through them. It's like looking in a fun-house mirror, the lines bending in a supple, constantly moving flow.

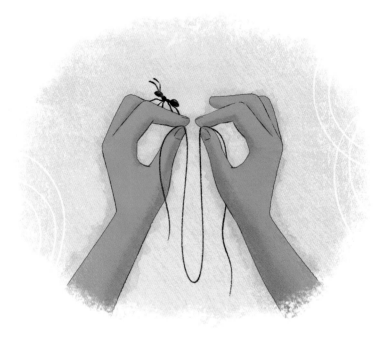

Out of nowhere, a hole opens in the air, rings of sparks zinging within and the space outside it dipping inward as though dropping over a waterfall. You clutch your guide's hand, the one who is leading the tesser.

But as you are pulled through, you are filled

with doubts. Are you really the right person for this quest? What if you fail? You'll let everyone down. This is your chance to prove yourself, but are you ready? Surely there is someone smarter or more talented who would be a better choice.

Then you can see nothing but a blinding light, and you are spun relentlessly—nothing beneath you, nothing behind you, nothing in front of you. Your stomach swoops and drops. If you could open your mouth, you'd be sick, but the air is moving too fast for you to get your jaws apart.

Two giant, invisible rollers steam over you as you spiral—squeezing your fingers, your arms, your head, chest, and legs.

You can't breathe. You can't even blink.

What is happening? Where are you? What happened to your guide's hand? What if you get caught here, forever stuck in this awful limbo with no one beside you? Could you wind up lost in time, no way to break—

With a sickening lurch, you're free.

Gasping, you fill your lungs with sweet delicious air, the purest you've ever tasted. Your body aches as though it's been wrung out like a towel. You fear you might turn into a puddle if not for the solid surface cradling your back.

Pain digs deeper than your muscles, into your very bones. Behind your closed eyelids, the world still spins, threatening to tip you over the edge.

Taking a deep breath—fighting past the stabbing of your lungs—you focus on the ground beneath you. You can do this. You made it.

A riot of smells rushes into your nose—things you can't even identify, though they're floral in some way. Plus that zing of air, reminiscent of untainted oxygen.

Everything still hurts, but the dizzying rush slows like a train arriving at the platform. When you're sure it's safe, you force your eyes open.

The sky above you is a vibrant turquoise. Puffy purple clouds drift past.

You're not on Earth any longer.

chapter ten

uriel

While there are individual living beings who embody the Light, there are also some entire worlds that act as its protectors and conduits. Uriel is one such planet, a world with unparalleled natural beauty that serves as a beacon of the Light to all living things. It was no accident that Uriel was the first place Dr. Alex Murry tessered to, and in their search for him, it is the first place Meg and the others visit, as well.

Wind prickled along the flowers on Uriel, ruffling their petals. Giggling, the flowers leaned closer together. In hushed tones, they chatted about the nearby river, who had been in such a grouchy mood that day—flinging himself up against the rocks. Anyone would think a storm had poured itself into him, but the last thunderstorm had been moons earlier. Uriel had moved into its peak summer season. The warmth of its sun soaked into the flowers' petals, not a hint of rain in the breeze. Dancing in delight, the flowers broke out in a riot of colors—splashes of orange, violet, and blue. No grumpy river could dampen their mood.

On the outer edges of the field, a flower sent up a warning.

Somebody—no, several somebodies were coming. The flowers turned to sense the newcomers.

Shining light emanated from three figures cresting the hill.

The elementals were back!

Whirling bright yellow in joy, the flowers turned to welcome them. But why were they in such strange shapes? And who was that with them?

Three additional creatures moved beside them. Their stalks split in two at the bottom, and they had two leaves that drooped down their sides. They looked just like that other odd visitor the flowers had had. But where that one had had bristles all over his face, these only had fuzz popping out the tops of their heads. The muted, drab colors of their petals, leaves, and stems made the flowers sad. Were they so full of despair that they couldn't show joy?

One of the unknown creatures raced toward them, its leaves outspread. Flushing purple in alarm, the flowers plucked themselves up and flew backward. The figure stopped, its face turned up toward them, part of it opening into a circle.

Having put enough distance between themselves and the figure, the flowers drifted back to the rich soil, digging their roots in, yet coiled and ready to spring out again if needed.

What could these creatures want? Where had they come from? Didn't they know proper etiquette?

One of the elementals, cloaked in that bizarre shape, nudged the brash intruder closer, buzzing in her ear. The flowers leaned away.

Hello, the oldest elemental waved, her aura flashing green in greeting and a sign of peace.

Walking forward, the youngest tilted her head to hear their concerns.

With a pulse of colors, the flowers asked: *Are these creatures friends of yours?*

The elemental assured them they were and nodded in understanding when the blooms shivered in relief. They'd heard rumors of places where plants were not treated gently, where large plates crushed petals between them and sharp blades sheared the stems in half.

The elemental brushed gently along a flower's face and the whole pack flickered bright pink in joy as a rush of energy bolted through the flower, down to the ground, and up the surrounding stems.

The curly-topped figure edged closer and held something out to them. What was it? Should they go see? They wouldn't know unless some of them ventured over.

After a heated exchange, several of the flowers valiantly lifted up and fluttered closer.

The shiny object on the creature's appendage

glinted in the light. They couldn't understand what it intended. A discordant flood of sickly gray seeped from the figure. Well, if she was confused and full of doubt, they certainly couldn't help it.

Shrugging, the flowers leapt into the air and spun down the valley seeking warmer—and less depressing—pastures.

Within a few moments, the flowers were preoccupied with figuring out which tree was casting too much shade and jostling one another for the best spots. As soon as they were settled, they chattered at the trees and river about the strange beings the elementals had brought with them and how uncouth they had been—gesticulating and rushing around, stamping the ground carelessly.

From where they'd left the creatures, a fiery blast of longing beamed into the sky. The planet responded, all the rocks, rivers, and plants singing. The flowers lifted their faces to the sky and added their voices to the chorus, blending perfectly into the harmony of Uriel.

This was what made Uriel the best world in the universe—a beautiful planetwide symphony of every part working together. For all Camazotz's closeness, the IT had not yet been able to pierce through the pure love Uriel's beings had for one another.

The flowers didn't know it, but the IT had not really tried yet. The waterlogged planet was a low priority.

A shadow crossed over their faces. It was the youngest elemental, back in her favorite form! The flowers passed a rainbow of colors through their petals as she flew by.

Bunching together, the flowers followed her to the shoreline, peering up in curiosity as the elemental showed the strangers the awful planet looming above them.

Suddenly, a cry of panic disrupted Uriel's song. A shape was plummeting through the sky. It wasn't the elemental.

Why wasn't it spreading its petals to fly? Did it

not know how to float on the air currents? Oh dear, oh dear.

Springing into the air, the flowers extended their petals to their utmost reach, forming a circle under the figure. Its weight crushed against them, but more flowers pushed up from underneath to add support.

Together, they drifted down and placed the figure carefully on the sand. It wasn't the doubtful curly-topped one, or the smallest one, who was full of wonder. This one radiated its thanks.

The flowers bobbed their heads in acknowledgment as the elementals and other figures joined them on the beach. After some buzzing between them, the curly-topped one turned to them, no longer surrounded by a pale gray but a confident crimson instead. Again she proffered the silver gem.

But this time when they leaned closer, the flowers could see in its center a picture of the earlier

visitor—the one who had fallen down upon getting to Uriel and let out bellows of victory before leaping past them. Waving in excitement, the flowers rearranged themselves, tinting themselves red, orange, and blue.

The figure tilted her head before racing to a nearby hill and climbing it. From higher up, she could see the full pattern the flowers made, and they nodded happily as she bounced up and down, rays of yellow flowing out of her.

Her colors shifted, asking if their visitor was still there, on Uriel, and if they knew where he was.

No, they didn't know. Hanging their heads in pity, they wished they had more answers for the figures. The visitor had vanished as abruptly as he'd appeared. If he were anywhere on Uriel, they'd know it, but no whisper of him had reached the flowers since he'd left.

There was nothing more they could do to help. Still, the figures thanked the flowers before the elementals whisked them away.

Chapter Eleven
The Happy Medium

*In a universe pulled in every possible direction,
one of the most difficult things to do is find a
balance. The Happy Medium understands better
than most that the only way to fight against
the Darkness is to truly know how light and
dark exist in the universe at the same time.*

B lack dirt smudged his shoes as the Happy
Medium scuffled along the path. He'd have
to wipe them off before entering his cave. He
didn't want any extra dust sullying the space
he'd worked so hard to perfect. With a nervous
glance up at the sky, the Happy Medium ducked
into the mouth of the cave.

His quick and steady hands brushed off his

shoes. One final peek outside reassured him—the IT had not found him yet.

"Can't be thinking about the IT, no, not good, not good. Will give me indigestion," he muttered to himself.

Hopping up onto the closest beam, the first of many stone pillars he'd hauled in to place around the cavern, he slid down to the next bridge. From there he flipped over to a standalone column. Gently, he tapped one of the amber spheres stacked there.

Instantly, a golden light filled the cavern, making the vast space seem cozy and snug.

Yes, he missed the broad expanses of sky where he could watch the scudding of clouds and the whirling of stars, but the cave was a good home. A safe home. No danger there.

The last time he'd enjoyed the sunset had been when Whatsit had last visited. They'd had a pleasant walk along the ridge overlooking the valley.

"What a wonderful view," Whatsit had said.

Giant rock formations thrust up through low-lying clouds, their gray stone dotted with scraggly, hardy trees and patches of moss. Teetering on the tops of many of the rocks were horizontal stones; it looked like someone had placed a hat atop each one.

Amber globes in all different sizes were scattered everywhere, an inner light from each one reflecting onto the clouds and suffusing the entire planet with a delightful warm glow.

"Although," Whatsit had continued, "you really should let me take you to Uriel. Now there is a planet with marvelous vistas. The variety in the flora is incredible and the water is a pure blue. We could soar through the giant flower pods, skim over the river . . ."

"You forget, Whatsit," Happy had answered, "I can see Uriel anytime I'd like. All I have to do is focus my mind's eye."

He'd run his finger over an amber stone, a light inside it sparking at his touch. In the air between them, a vision of Uriel hovered, a soft tune floating out of the scene.

Mrs. Whatsit smiled sadly. "You know it's not the same. You're not *feeling* the wind against your face or inhaling the sweetness of the flowers, and this song is just a pale echo of the glorious notes you can hear when you're really there."

Happy nodded. But for him, the risks were not worth the reward. Not anymore, not with the IT spreading.

"True, Whatsit, true. Yet you must admit, here I can see anything from the comfort of home. I needn't get my clothes sandy, and no pollen lands in my hair."

Whatsit's mouth twisted into an amused half smile. He suspected she knew his real reason: the fear lurking in his heart.

"Happy, you're ridiculous," she'd said.

He'd let the vision of Uriel go, moving farther along a narrow stone bridge. On the other side, an enormous solitary rock reached for the sky, the entrance to a cavern carved in its side.

"No, Whatsit, what I am is perfectly balanced. Not too silly, not too serious, not too brave, not too frightened. I know you love to travel, to dive into new experiences and worlds, but I feel happiest here, with my rocks for company. This is the place where I feel centered and at peace."

"I still think you're missing out," Whatsit had teased. "But if that's the way you want it, fine."

A tingle skittered up his arm as she brushed against him, the narrow bridge forcing them closer together. His insides somersaulted, throwing off his equilibrium. Happy fell behind, letting her go first. He inhaled deeply, closed his eyes, and paused for a moment, sticking out one leg to focus his mind on his body. Balance returned, he blinked his eyes open to see Whatsit studying him, her head cocked to the side.

"Are you okay, Happy?" Soft concern for him— *for him!*—wove out of her.

What was that odd squirming in his chest? Maybe he needed more air.

"Oh, yes, just fine, thank you for asking." Shaking his head, he smiled and followed her down the path. They'd climbed to the top of the rock and watched the sunset. As the sun dropped below the horizon, light painted the clouds bold oranges and pinks, gradually giving way to deep purples and blues. Once the sun was truly gone, the amber rocks took over, their lights scattered like stars on the ground.

Whatsit had clapped her hands in joy. Happy's cheeks ached from his answering smile. She hadn't stayed much longer.

A week after her visit, he'd been skipping through the stones, searching for a new beam to form a stairway he was working on, when a dark shadow had skimmed over the ground. Happy had frozen, one foot in the air.

Tentatively, he'd peered upward. Against the bright sun, a smudge of nothingness drifted by, moving faster than the clouds.

Goosebumps rose on Happy's skin and claws sank into his heart. Panicked, he'd scrambled into the cave and stayed there until the next day, too petrified to move.

At dawn, Happy had painstakingly collected each amber globe and lugged them all into the cavern. Couldn't have them shining out there, tempting the IT to come investigate. Nothing to see there; nope, this planet was just a lump of rock, not worth the IT's time.

That had been too close a call. Ever since then, he'd stayed inside as much as possible, slipping out only when absolutely necessary, usually at night or on cloudy days.

"Ah, what shall I look at today?" Happy asked himself.

He bounded from one pillar to another, finally landing on one in the middle of a circle of amber stones. As one wobbled, he reached out and, with a featherlight touch, eased it into a stronger alignment. There—that was just the right angle, and now it would be secure.

On the plus side, there was no wind in the cavern to disrupt his towers. Happy believed in looking at the positives. One had to, to balance out all the sadness in the universe.

"Something happy, I think." Happy raised one foot to rest against his other leg and pressed his hands together in front of his stomach. There was the faintest rustle as his fingers brushed his silk waistband, then blissful silence reigned.

Closing his eyes, Happy concentrated.

Two big brown pools blinked into view. Happy zoomed back until they clarified into the eyes of a furry otter. She was resting on her mother's tummy, both of them floating in a cold inlet. The mother chattered at her, then used her paws to slick down the baby's fur. Wriggling, the baby nuzzled deeper into her mother, heat flowing between their bodies.

Happy sighed in contentment. Unconditional love—there was no greater force in the universe.

BOOM! *Clink, clink, clink.*

Happy's eyes shot open at the sound of several amber globes crashing to the ground and rolling away. His foot stamped to the floor.

"What's that? Who's there? Which way?" Happy whirled, scanning the cavern. "Unpleasant sounds amongst my pleasant things?"

Flipping through the air, he grabbed hold of a beam and swung to an outcropping. From there, he could see a group traipsing into his sanctuary.

"Uninvited guests. How upsetting," he muttered.

Mrs. Whatsit, Mrs. Who, and Mrs. Which were each escorting a human child along the series of beams he'd arranged. The children's emotions were bubbling uncontrollably, setting Happy's stomach roiling.

Children. They were so . . . not calm.

Resigning himself to a distressing visit, Happy strode out. "Don't touch anything!" he bellowed.

Oh, his precious globes and precisely balanced beams! He had a feeling they would not remain in place for long.

Happy's premonition proved all too true. The humans were clumsy, not mean, but they slipped off beams and knocked over stones. It soon became clear the celestial beings had brought them in search of the father of two of them—Meg and Charles Wallace.

Happy would much rather have shown the girl frolicking puppies, but she was determined to seek her father. So Happy talked her through centering herself and pushed his energy toward her, helping her open up her vision. Together, they traced the thread of Meg's love, bringing up images of her and her father, then how her father had tessered—the world around him wrinkling as he slipped through time and space.

Meg wavered, and globes and rocks began to fall, shaken loose by her emotions.

"Stay focused!" Happy entreated.

Redoubling her efforts, Meg concentrated, casting out across the universe to find where her father was now. Happy gritted his teeth as the pillars and beams of his cavern continued to cascade down and the amber globes toppled. He could not blame Meg for being passionate. She had not yet learned how to control her emotions. The mission took precedence over his masterpiece.

A blank room appeared, lit by a blaring violet light. Trapped within, Meg's father pounded against the opaque glass walls. Now they knew he was alive, but caged. There weren't enough details, nothing to pinpoint his location.

"Try to see where you are. What planet? What solar system—" Happy began.

He guided Meg's mind to pull back, beyond the room, out of the building, out of the city.

Out, out, out, until they were suspended in space, gazing at a dark planet.

Camazotz.

"No!" Meg screamed.

With a *pop*, the vision burst and Meg tumbled from the last standing beam. Happy dove to catch her, scooping her into his arms. He settled her on the ground, patting her head.

He hated that he'd been a part of showing her such terrible news. Camazotz! The IT had her father.

Yet Meg's next words were not about her troubles.

"I'm so sorry. I broke your home," she said, gazing around at the scattered stalagmites and rubble.

How sweet of her to be concerned. Happy felt a gentle tug on his heart. Maybe children weren't so irksome.

"I'll rebuild," he said. "It'll give me something to do."

Perhaps he'd shift the rocks so there would be a bridge to that outcropping on the far wall he'd always had to leap to before. Happy's mind began clicking through possibilities.

"Or you could leave it be," Mrs. Whatsit said as she and the others joined them from the rock overhang they'd been sheltering under. "Come out of the cave," she cajoled.

"Maybe one day," Happy said.

Not yet, though. He wasn't ready yet. There was still so much darkness out there. But maybe, if the children before him fulfilled the potential shining in them . . . Maybe then, if the Darkness was driven back, he'd watch a sunset again. Maybe with Mrs. Whatsit by his side.

While Happy's abilities as a seer let him show people the universe, it was up to them to decide what to do with the information. Meg was pushing hard for a rescue mission straight to Camazotz. *What a disaster that would be,* Happy thought. *Imagine going up against the IT with no training!* No preparation! Mrs. Which and the other, wiser minds prevailed. They'd return to Earth, connect with Meg's mother, and come up with a plan.

He waved farewell as his visitors tessered away. Once they'd vanished, he turned back to his cavern.

"Big mess, big mess," he tutted. Exhaling deeply, he set about righting the stalagmites, then adjusting and readjusting their placement.

Happy had to stand back every few moves, analyzing the space from all angles. With minuscule tweaks and huge shifts, he slowly rebuilt his home.

As he picked up an amber stone, he ran his hand along its smooth surface. It warmed to his touch. Maybe he'd just check in on them . . . see how they were getting on. . . .

Bracing himself for inevitable anxiety, Happy closed his eyes and pictured Meg, that brave, stubborn girl full of spirit, whose heart was bigger than she knew. If anyone could find a way to outdo the IT, perhaps it was her.

Mrs. Which

Mrs. Which is the leader and most powerful
of the three celestial beings aiding Meg on her
journey. But no power is infinite, and even Mrs.
Which has boundaries she cannot cross.

She was fading, unable to hold on any longer. The Darkness on Camazotz was too suffocating. There was no Light, and without Light, she and Mrs. Who and Mrs. Whatsit could not last. They weren't supposed to be there. Not like this. Well, no matter; they were there now, and they'd have to make the best of it.

Drawing herself up, she stared hard at Meg, Calvin, and Charles Wallace. The three warriors were so young, and now they'd be on their own, up against the purest evil in the universe.

"Stay together," she told them. The IT was very powerful and manipulative. Together, they might have a chance, but if the IT could divide them, it would overwhelm them one by one.

Meg bit her lip, so worried, so guilt-ridden. She had been the one to wrench control of their last tesser away from Mrs. Which—her burning desire to save her father sweeping them all up, barreling through the field around Camazotz Mrs. Which could not penetrate, and dumping them all on the surface. This hadn't been the plan. Meg had not intended to do this, and now she was beginning to see how much danger they were in, but she didn't know the half of it.

If only Mrs. Which could show Meg how strong she really was, how amazing and resilient. Meg just needed to accept herself as she was—not try to conform. Oh, how the IT might be able to tempt her!

Meg wanted to belong, to be liked, even though her differences were what made her so incredible.

Reaching out his hand, Calvin rested it on Meg's shoulder. He was such a sweet boy, and so trusting, always looking for the best in others. She hoped the IT wouldn't sink its tentacles into him, sucking him into the toxic thoughts the IT blasted into the universe. To see him poisoned like that would hurt Mrs. Which. Although she wouldn't be there to see it. The air around her was harder to breathe, the planet trying to force her away.

With her last strength, she fixed her gaze on Charles Wallace. His mind was unique for a human in its perceptiveness, but that sensitivity and ability to read others would be something the IT would covet for itself. The IT would want him most of all. While Charles Wallace's soul was pure and full of love for his family, there were still weaknesses there: a bruise from never having known his father—for that abandonment at so young an age—and his supreme

confidence in himself combined with his intelligence could be a liability. He'd believe he was smart enough to outwit the IT and withstand its assault on his mind. He might even allow the IT inside on purpose, to try to see what lay at its core.

Only there was nothing there but a warped evil that could never be redeemed. Mrs. Which had grappled closely with the IT herself and was certain the IT was not something that could be reasoned with or fixed. There was no bringing the IT to the Light.

Invisible hands tore her apart as Mrs. Which began to dissolve, her being dissipating into particles. With her last moments on Camazotz, she willed the three children to resist the IT with all their hearts.

She was everywhere and nowhere, her essence scattered as she was pulled through the dark fog around the planet. Smoke clogged her vision, smothered her senses.

Then she was out in space, the weight lifted from her. Stars beamed a welcome to her, filling her with their light. Slowly, the pieces of her stitched back together. At her side, Mrs. Who and Mrs. Whatsit were reborn, as well.

They were all jittery, shaken by their time in a place absent of light and hope.

"Will they be okay?" Mrs. Whatsit asked anxiously, her spirit twisting and turning in consternation. "It is worse there than I had imagined. So very dark and dismal, and the taste of the air—*ugh*. I'm not sure I'll ever get rid of it. They're so young and inexperienced. What if the IT . . . what if the IT takes them, too? What if we made it worse by bringing them into this?"

Light shone from Mrs. Which, the gentle beams caressing her companions in reassurance.

"We must have faith in them. Experience and years are not everything. They have a will to win, and the bonds of love between them are strong. We have given them everything we can and although this is not what we intended, remember that the Light always finds a way."

"'People are like stained glass windows,'" Mrs.

Who spoke up. "'They sparkle and shine when the sun is out, but when the darkness sets in, their true beauty is revealed only if there is a light from within.' Kübler-Ross, Swiss."

"Those three have great light within. I believe that they will face the dark and prevail," Mrs. Which agreed.

Mrs. Whatsit's spirit twitched. "Is there nothing else we can do?" she fretted. "They have much light in them, but I've never felt anything like that place." A shudder ran through her.

"All we can do now is wait and watch," Mrs. Which said gently.

"'When a train goes through a tunnel and it gets dark, you don't throw away the ticket and jump off. You sit still and trust the engineer.' ten Boom, Dutch," Mrs. Who proclaimed. She gathered her spirit close, like a quilt.

Mrs. Which studied her, a feeling of warmth blossoming within. "Why don't we go to Ixchel while we wait?" she suggested.

Mrs. Who brightened at the mention of her former home. The planet was close by and would be a good place to bring the children and Mr. Murry to recover once they broke free of the IT.

"Yes!" Mrs. Whatsit squealed. "What a brilliant idea! You are always so wise, Mrs. Which."

Mrs. Who, Mrs. Whatsit, and Mrs. Which linked energies, colored lights swirling around them.

Looking at the dark, hulking shape of Camazotz before them, Mrs. Which whispered, "We will see you soon, warriors."

Chapter thirteen
Ixchel

*Meg Murry is surrounded by empathetic beings
on her journey across the universe, but none
as deeply soothing and understanding as the
being known as Aunt Beast. Part of a race of
beings who thrive on the serene frozen planet of
Ixchel, Aunt Beast accepts Meg for who she is,
all her faults, all her strengths, all the same.*

Icy snow crunched under her feet as Aunt Beast
trooped across the plains of Ixchel. The cold
felt refreshing, her thick hair insulating her
against the frigid air. From the warmth radiat-
ing off them, she could sense her herd around her,
all of them moving toward their playing grounds.

A hilltop lay ahead; the steep slope on its other

side made for the best sledding on the planet. Next to her, Uncle Wild sent out a chuckle, picking up on her anticipation. His arm brushed against her, tickling her with patience.

As they reached the crest of the hill, she sensed the ground dropping away below them. At the bottom lay several pools, their underground thermals sending up powerful ripples of energy.

Wheee! Aunt Beast released her excitement to the minds of her herd mates as she curled into a ball and let gravity pull her downhill.

Faster and faster she whirled, the motion whipping each strand of her fur. At the last moment, she pivoted, braking to a sudden stop right at the edge of a pool. Snow puffed up against her foot, spilling over into the water.

The ground vibrated under her as the others pelted down the hill after her until they jostled against her in a giddy cluster. One at a time, they each took turns dipping through the steam into the luxurious water and hopping back out again, the sensation of hot and cold smacking their skin.

Their journey back to their dens was slower, their contentment easing their movements. Half-way home, they sensed the three elementals on the ridge above them, anxiously watching the sky. Aunt Beast sent a beam of reassurance to them, and Mrs. Who responded with a grateful wave in return.

Aaaaaaaaahhhhhhh! A primal mental scream rent the atmosphere as an amateur tesserer opened a hole in the valley below the plains. Three figures staggered through, the largest pushing the two smaller ones ahead of him.

All the hairs on Aunt Beast perked up, tasting the air. All three were in terrible pain, but one was worse off than the others, her spirit crushed under a tremendous weight.

Urgency driving her faster, Aunt Beast led the charge of her herd toward the newcomers. Only the elementals outpaced her, arriving first.

As Aunt Beast arrived, the other figures were pleading with the troubled girl, whose anguish was destroying her from the inside out. Their worry pulsed through the air as the girl coughed and gasped in pain.

Gently, Aunt Beast nudged her way through the group. She sensed surprise and fear from the two human watchers, but left it to the elementals to explain. The girl, Meg, had more pressing needs.

With unerring arms, though she could not see or hear as the humans did, relying instead on mental connections, Aunt Beast scooped Meg up and cradled her close, rounding herself around the girl like a snowball.

Aunt Beast directed her warmth into her, both physically and mentally, for there was much to heal.

Meg's battle with the IT had not gone well. The IT had nearly destroyed her, squeezing her flat. Worse to Meg, though, was what she saw as her father's betrayal—tessering away from Camazotz without Charles Wallace. Meg's brother, the person

she loved and sought to protect most in the world, had been caught in the IT's snare.

What Meg did not realize yet was that if her father had tried to bring Charles Wallace with them, he might have inadvertently ended up killing the boy instead now that the IT had entangled itself in his mind. There would still be a chance to rescue him, but only if Meg let herself heal.

Aunt Beast rocked back and forth, purring to soothe the roiling of Meg's soul. Rage, betrayal, and guilt lashed through her. Aunt Beast couldn't understand it. Why did Meg think she was not good enough, that she had failed her brother? Meg's love for him was clear and indisputable.

Purring louder, Aunt Beast calmed Meg's wild thoughts. She needed to rest, to release her anger, or she would succumb to the IT, as well. Aunt Beast broadcast the message that she was safe and all would be well over and over, underscored by her love for the girl, hoping to ease the child into sleep.

Meg's heart slowed its frantic beat and her mind

quieted for the moment, but she would need more care. The immediate danger was past, but if Meg was to return to challenge the IT for her brother's freedom, she would first need to learn to accept herself. The poor child was too self-critical.

Mrs. Who could sense Meg's psychic pain, as well. "'The best and most beautiful things in the world cannot be seen or even touched—they must be felt with the heart.' Keller, American," she said. From her own heart, love poured out, wrapping Meg and Aunt Beast.

Aunt Beast tsked in agreement. Humans often focused on what they could see and touch, forgetting that the most powerful thing in the universe was intangible, invisible. Love was not a color, a picture, or a texture. She wouldn't be able to study or hold it, but love could heal Meg's wounds.

Fortunately, there was no one better than Aunt Beast at unconditional love. She would show this girl how much she was loved . . . just as she was, no changes necessary. What a remarkable girl, indeed, thought Aunt Beast, sensing Meg's aura as she slumbered.

With a cluck to the herd from Aunt Beast, the creatures began the trek to their dens, escorting the humans with them. Tucked tight against Aunt Beast's stomach, Meg slept, her dreams infused with the love Aunt Beast devoted to her.

You are safe, little love, Aunt Beast told her. *Everything will be okay.*

chapter fourteen
Tessering Well

*The discovery of tessering by Drs. Alex and Kate
Murry was founded in mathematics. But Meg
discovers that to master the technique, every piece
of the universe must be considered to truly unlock
the potential of all matter. Where her father and
mother realized love was a force that needed to be
accounted for in their initial equations and explorations
of tessering, Meg realizes both the light and the
dark that exist within every living being need to be
acknowledged for tessering to occur. When she finds
her own balance, she is finally able to tesser well.*

B eneath your feet, the ground trembles, but
you sway in tune with it—your feet steadied
by an invisible force. Last time, you didn't
hear it, but music fills the air—a soaring

melody with low and high notes weaving together in an intricate rhythm.

The air before you shimmers like millions of little prisms catching the light and fracturing it into rainbows. In the center, a circular doorway opens inward, light from your world spilling over the edge and merging with a kaleidoscope of colored lines dancing along the inside walls of the portal.

This time, you know who you are, and you are happy with you—faults and all. It is through your flaws that you learn, grow, and become more. It is through your faults that you know when someone loves you, and you love someone else for their flaws, too. No person is perfect, nor should you be. You should just *be*.

Your body is gently cradled by the invisible force, as though you've been wrapped in a flannel blanket by a giant, and you are carried forward. As you zoom through, the motion tugging at your hair, you have all the fun of a roller coaster without any of the jerkiness or fear of falling. Your heart lifts in joy and you release all your cares.

Bubbles of happiness press against your insides as though you were filled with seltzer water, and the sweet scent of honeysuckle tickles your nose. Later, you may wish you could feel like this all the time, but here in the moment, there is not even room to worry about it ending or about later; you are just here and now and euphoric.

Your feet touch down on green grass, leaves rustle overhead, and fireflies flicker through the yard. Someone somewhere is having a barbecue, and the tangy smell wafts on a breeze that is the perfect coolness after a hot day.

As you are released from the invisible hand, the tesseract closes behind you with a subtle *whoosh*, and the music goes with it. Yet your skin still tingles, and overlaying everything you look at is the light of its energy—each individual blade of grass sparkling, while the willow tree has veins of light

running through its trunk and branches down to each golden leaf.

Gradually, that fades and the real world's colors and lines return, but the joy lingers.

This world is a beautiful, amazing place.

This is your world.

You are home.

Chapter Fifteen
HOME

The azure sky was broken only by striations of white, the clouds a soft dabbing of a paintbrush on the canvas above. Nearby, birds chirped, their calls rebounding off the flat expanse of the lake.

Lying back on the picnic blanket, Meg tilted her face up to the sun. It was a relief to be back where the sunshine felt as it should, not like that horrible fake stuff on Camazotz.

"How are you doing, sweetie?" Meg's mom dropped down next to her. Fortinbras came panting up, as well, and stretched out on the grass under a nearby tree.

"I am exultant, as Charles Wallace would say," Meg said.

Her mom smiled. "As you should be. You did an amazing thing, my dear. Only . . ."

"I know, I know," Meg said. "No more tessering without a parent."

Meg didn't think she could tesser again on her own anyway. Honestly, she had no desire to go anywhere anytime soon. She was enjoying life there too much. For the first time in a long time, everything felt right.

Down at the shoreline, her dad and Charles Wallace were busy building a sand city, complete with bridges over canals, towers, and a domed observatory. They were both so meticulous that Meg had to laugh. Right then they were debating which little round rock should go on which building. Calvin, who'd joined the Murrys for the day, was farther down the beach, unearthing more pebbles for them.

Ever since his return, her father had thrown himself into being a parent, eager to soak up as

much time with them as he could to make up for everything he'd missed. He'd begged Meg to reenact her fifth-grade play performance (she'd been a tree, but he didn't care), and he'd delved through all of Charles Wallace's drawings and hung up a gallery of them in the living room. They had family breakfasts and dinners, game nights on Thursdays, and movie nights on Fridays.

When NASA had called, he'd barely acknowledged them, although he had given Meg's mom a complete rundown on their journey and they'd searched the star charts as a family to find possible galaxies where Uriel and Ixchel might be. He'd promised them he'd never tesser again unless they all agreed to it. After three weeks, journalists and newscasters had given up on getting his story out of him and wandered away in pursuit of new subjects. The Murrys and Calvin had talked it over and decided the world wasn't quite ready to meet the rest of the universe just yet, and they didn't want anyone accidentally tessering into the path of the IT. So for now, they were keeping the truth to themselves.

"It's still hard to believe sometimes," Meg's mom whispered, her eyes on the two builders.

Meg knew what she meant. Some days she'd arrive in the kitchen and startle to see her dad there, cooking eggs or flipping pancakes. The sight of his shoes in the hallway would pull her up short, and she wished she could bottle the rumble of his voice as he read to Charles Wallace, part of her not fully trusting it wouldn't disappear again. Yet the biggest change was in her mom.

Meg hadn't realized just how much pressure had been weighing on her mother until she saw her relax. She'd never been uptight or anything and had rolled with every swerve and obstacle along the way for the past four years, but as soon as Meg's dad came back, her spirit seemed lighter. She laughed more, a full-bodied, uncontrollable laugh, and she would dance around the kitchen as she cooked. Meg would find her snuggled on the couch with a novel— something she hadn't had time for in years—and she routinely sent their father out for groceries, claiming he owed her about six hundred trips or so.

"Yes, boss," Meg's father would say, saluting her as he headed for the door.

Meg reached over and squeezed her mom's hand. "We're really okay now," she said.

"We're more than okay, thanks to you," her mom replied, squeezing back.

"She's a true hero," Calvin said, walking back toward Meg and her mother.

Meg felt heat rising to her cheeks and she ducked her head. "You are, too," she told Calvin.

"You're both terrific. Now, if you'll excuse me, I think I'll go see if those two architects down there can tear themselves away from their city planning long enough to eat lunch with us." Meg's mom stood and surreptitiously winked at Meg before floating down to the water.

Calvin flopped down next to Meg. "I could eat," he said.

"Ha!" Meg laughed. Calvin was always hungry,

she'd discovered, even right after a meal. It was as though his body burned calories by smiling, so of course his stomach was eternally empty.

They shared a smile. Then Meg pulled the basket toward her and handed him a jelly sandwich and an apple before picking out her own, as well.

"How's track going?" Meg asked.

"Really well," Calvin answered. "My dad's coming around to it. That whole 'competing against yourself' idea appealed to him, so he gets that aspect of it, and I think he's genuinely impressed at my times."

"As he should be—you're a blur out there on the field!"

Calvin smiled at her praise, blushing. "Thanks. If you want to know my secret, sometimes I picture us back on Camazotz with the IT ripping the ground and trees to shreds behind us."

They both shuddered at the memory. After experiencing that, Meg felt extra empathy for those living in tornado country.

"That would get me moving, too," she said.

For the next few minutes, the crunching of their food was the only sound. By the water's edge, Meg's dad and brother had cajoled her mom into holding a stick with a rock on top as they packed sand around it into the shape of one of the flower pods they'd seen on Uriel.

"Bet you nobody else in our class has logged as many miles," Calvin joked.

"Or flown on the back of a furry ribbon creature," Meg added.

"Nor trekked through anywhere as cold as Ixchel." He shivered.

"Nobody else has seen the beauties of the universe or battled its darkness. They'll never know what we went through," Meg said. Her voice ached a little. She knew nobody would believe them, but if she could, she'd shout about the dangers of the IT through a megaphone from the top of a cafeteria table and paint them all pictures of the incredible landscapes and creatures beyond their planet. But

nobody could really fully appreciate it until they'd
been there themselves.

"But we'll know," Calvin said softly. He brushed
off his hands and then gently reached for hers.

Sparks burst under her skin at his touch. After
a few minutes, they settled to a steady glow, like a
candle. Out of all the people across all the galaxies,

they'd found each other. He saw her for who she was, and she knew him better than anyone else could. After all, they'd been to the edge of the universe and back.

Something tickled her finger. Peering down, she saw an ant crawling over her hand, crossing from her brown skin to Calvin's white and back again where their fingers were intertwined. He was studying it, too.

"Must be on its way to the crumbs," he said.

As it dipped down onto the blanket, Meg looked up at Calvin with a grin. "Shall we help it along?"

Laughing, the two of them wrinkled the blanket so the ant could step from its spot to a juicy morsel of sandwich in the blink of an eye.

"You're welcome," Meg whispered, happy to give the ant its own sort of tessering experience.

"What's so funny?" Mr. Murry called.

"Just . . . the magic of the fifth dimension," Meg answered.

She stood up and pulled Calvin to his feet next to her. "Come on," she said. "We've got a planet to build."

Whooping in joy, the two of them raced down to the beach, sand grains sifting between their toes and wind playing with their hair. Fortinbras lumbered to his feet and trundled after them, wearily amused at their wild movements. Mr. Murry swept Meg up and spun her around, making her shriek, as Mrs. Murry cued up a song on her phone. "Here Comes the Sun" began playing, the notes booming out of a portable speaker Calvin had brought from home.

The music soared as Meg, Calvin, and Charles Wallace chased each other through the sand and the Drs. Murry danced to the beat. No matter what darkness still lurked on Earth and in the universe, they had each other and would stick together, no matter what.